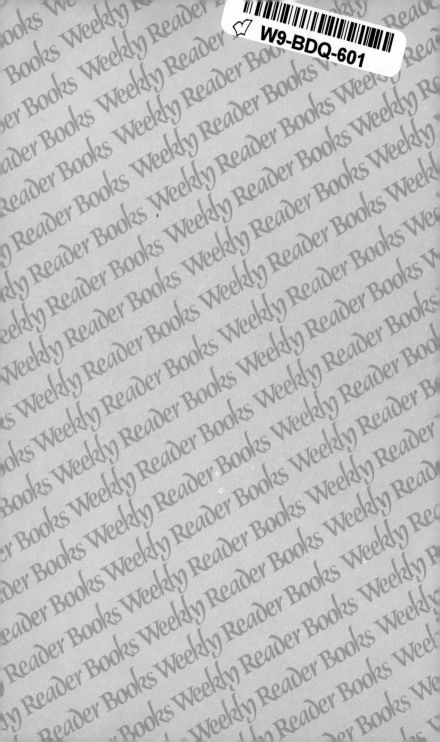

P.J.

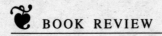 **BOOK REVIEW**

*Realism is the word for this natural
story of day-to-day fifth-grade living.*
from PARENTS' CHOICE MAGAZINE

Weekly Reader Books presents

Andrea Balis and Robert Reiser

Houghton Mifflin Company
Boston   1984

This book is a presentation of Weekly Reader Books.
Weekly Reader Books offers book clubs for children
from preschool through high school. For further
information write to: **Weekly Reader Books,**
4343 Equity Drive, Columbus, Ohio 43228.

Edited for Weekly Reader Books and published by
arrangement with Houghton Mifflin Company.

Library of Congress Cataloging in Publication Data

Balis, Andrea.
  P.J.

  For ages 8–12.
  Summary: A fifth grader whose reputation at home and
at school is too-"good" sets out to build a new image
with disastrous results.
  [1. Parent and child—Fiction. 2. Schools—Fiction]
I. Reiser, Robert. II. Title.
PZ7.B1982Pab   1984   [Fic]   83-26475
ISBN 0-395-36006-4

For George and Sandy

our husband and wife

P.J.

✎ ONE

JESSIE'S TEAM WAS ONE RUN BEHIND, AND THEY JUST *HAD* to win—she and Nancy had bragged to everybody at lunch that they would. Soon it would start to get dark and the game would be over, and they would lose!

It was Jessie's turn to kick. She walked up to the plate very slowly, remembering to concentrate and keep her eye on the ball. Her hands were sweaty, but that didn't matter because in kickball you just need your feet. She took a couple of deep breaths. Breathing is important but you don't want to take too many breaths because that makes you dizzy. She was ready.

1

Her feet were ready. She waited for the ball.

Just as Fred was about to pitch to her, he stopped, giggling. Jessie turned around. Right behind her stood Ben Carney, the meanest boy in her class—maybe in the whole fifth grade. He was making ears over her head.

"Get out of here," Nancy yelled. Nancy was her best friend and she knew how much Jessie hated Ben. Also, Nancy was up next and she didn't want Ben hanging around either.

"You can't make me," Ben yelled back. "This is public property and I have just as much right to be here as you do."

"We got here first!" Jessie told him.

"I'm not stopping you from playing," Ben sneered. "And you can't stop me from watching."

"I can too," Jessie said.

"Oh, yeah?" Ben replied. "How?"

"Let's just play," Kenny yelled. "It's getting late."

"Yeah," Ben said, "Jessica has to hurry home and do her homework. If it isn't perfect, how can she be Mrs. Rogers's favorite little girl?"

"I am not!" Jessica screamed.

"Go away!" Nancy yelled again.

"No," Ben said. "I want to see Perfect Jessica's perfect kick."

"Ignore him," Nancy advised. "Only a retard or a third-grader makes ears."

Even though you aren't supposed to call people

retards, Jessie knew that Nancy was right. Ben just kept on teasing her. He was standing right behind her. She could practically feel his spit on her neck, because Ben splashed saliva around whenever he talked. She turned around to tell him that when Kenny pitched her the ball.

She forgot to breathe. She forgot to watch the ball. She forgot everything, and she missed—by about a mile.

"Oh, no!" Ben pretended to groan, as though his stomach hurt or something. "She missed the ball."

"Forget about him," Nancy yelled.

"Come on, Jessie, we need a run!" somebody else called out.

Jessie felt tears come into her eyes. She hated Ben so much. She clenched her teeth. She still had two more chances. She wasn't out yet. But Ben kept on shouting "P. J.! P. J.!" over and over, and she missed again. On her third try she kicked the ball with just her toe and it dribbled along the ground for about two feet. Gary simply picked it up and tagged her out.

"Too bad you guys have teacher's pet on your team. If Mrs. Rogers isn't watching, P. J. can't do anything," Ben called, getting onto his bike. "Maybe you won't get stuck with her next time." Before Jessie could say anything, Ben rode out of the park.

"It's my turn!" Nancy said, running over to home plate. "We haven't lost yet. We still have another out."

Nancy licked her lips, which is what she did when

she was really concentrating, instead of breathing. She leaned back as Kenny pitched the ball and she kicked it as hard as she could. You could hear the *thwank* all the way across the playground. Her kicking foot went up so high that she lost her balance and slipped in the mud, but that didn't matter. The ball bounced way over the outfield and nobody could get it. It went over the fence and out onto Hemlock Street. Nancy strolled around the bases and across home plate, covered with mud and grinning.

"Great kick!" Jessie made herself yell. After all, Nancy was her best friend and they had tied the score, which was a lot better than losing. Everybody was screaming and yelling and pounding Nancy on the back. Jessie did, too, but nobody paid any attention to her. After all, she had almost made them lose the game.

Nancy was running around looking for her stuff, which was scattered all over the park. Her notebook had pages sticking out of it, and when she picked it up they all fell into the mud. Jessie put them in a pile and handed them to Nancy, who just stuffed them back into her notebook, smearing mud all over everything. She stepped on the first page of her book report and got a sneaker print on it, but she didn't even seem to notice.

"You played great," Jessie said as they started walking home.

"Oh, well," Nancy said, trying to make Jessie feel

better, "except for the last time you were up, you played great, too."

"No, I didn't," Jessie said.

"It doesn't matter. It's just a game," Nancy answered.

"You sound like Miss Cranshaw." Jessie giggled. Miss Cranshaw was their gym teacher. She was about eighty and everyone said she wore bloomers. She was always lecturing them about how winning didn't matter, except that she yelled at you if you lost. She had a really high-pitched voice that sounded like one of those dogs that need ribbons to keep the hair out of their eyes. Except that Miss Cranshaw was practically bald.

"You know what your problem is . . ." Nancy began. "You pay too much attention to people like Ben, who are truly and absolutely idiots."

"But he was yelling in my ear," Jessie protested.

"You just have to ignore him. If you do, he'll stop," Nancy told her.

"He will not. He'll just yell louder."

"Let him. If he yells loud enough maybe he'll burst open." Nancy giggled. "And all that spit will come spilling out all over the ground."

"Yuck!"

"And even if it doesn't, he'll get a sore throat," Nancy said in a practical voice.

"That's true," Jessie agreed, "and he'll get pus on his tonsils."

"Probably," Nancy said cheerfully. "See you tomorrow."

Every night before dinner, Jessica's family sat around and talked together for a while. Her mother said that because they had such busy lives, it was especially important to spend some quiet time together. You were supposed to share your life, and stuff like that. You could even talk about your problems, but you had to discuss them; you couldn't complain or whine. Jessie couldn't always tell the difference, but her mother could.

Sometimes family hour was really great, when the three of them told funny stories and laughed, and sometimes it was really boring. The problem was, you couldn't tell ahead of time which it was going to be.

Tonight her father came in and gave her a big hug. He squeezed her hard, pushing the air right out of her, which sounds terrible but actually feels great.

"How was school?" he asked.

"Okay," Jessie told him. "We played kickball afterward."

"Who won?" her mother asked.

"We tied," Jessie said. "Nancy saved us. She kicked the ball so hard it practically went into orbit!"

"That would be a good science project," her father teased. "The first kickball satellite."

"I think you should stay away from satellite science projects for a while," her mother said.

"Uh uh." Jessie shook her head. "I'm going to do another one for next year. I've got it all figured out."

"This time just remember satellites aren't supposed to explode." Her father laughed.

"Well, maybe I won't say what it is till the last minute. Then if it does explode, I'll say it was supposed to be a bomb," Jessie said.

"That seems sensible," her mother said. "But whatever it is, we know yours will be the best project in the class."

"Did you have fun at work today?" Jessie asked her father.

He shook his head. "Plumbing supplies are not fun."

"What about flanges and grommets?" Jessie asked.

"Especially flanges and grommets." Her father pretended to be very serious.

"Even with Trudy around?" Jessie giggled. "If I had Trudy for my secretary, I would always have fun. The first thing I'd do if I had the kind of job where you get a secretary would be to hire her."

"Fortunately for you, Trudy already has a job," her mother reminded her.

Trudy was her father's secretary. She kept a pet hamster on her desk. Mostly it was in a cage, but sometimes Trudy let it out to play. The hamster's name was Godzilla, but of course it wasn't scary or anything. The last time Jessie visited her father at work she had let Godzilla out of his cage and then lost him. Finally, Trudy found him in the file cabinet, sitting there nibbling on papers. They decided not to tell Jessie's father because he didn't like hamsters very much. Trudy said she would just say the papers were lost. Jessie's father was used to that.

"What's for dinner?" asked her father.

"Fried chicken," answered her mother.

"Hurray!" Jessie cheered.

"And after dinner," her mom went on, "you'd better do your homework."

"But it's Friday!" Jessie complained.

"And you are going to Nancy's tomorrow," her mother reminded her. "And you know you won't do anything over there."

"But I can do it on Sunday!" Jessie said, almost whining.

"Then you will do a sloppy job," her mother said firmly. "If you do it now you can play for the whole weekend."

Nobody else in the whole world would be doing homework on a Friday night. But if she said that to her parents, they would just say they didn't care what other kids did, because she wasn't other kids.

When she got to Nancy's house the next afternoon, Mr. and Mrs. Helms were rushing around getting ready to go to a party.

"Dorothy, we're going to be late!" Nancy's father called up the stairs. Nancy and Jessie were helping Mrs. Helms get ready. They were trying to make her be on time, but it was very hard. For one thing, Mrs. Helms was always losing things. For example, she had eleven left-hand gloves. She said that she didn't know why, but she had always been that way. That was part of the reason it took her so long to get dressed. The other part was that she stopped in the middle of things to talk, and then she forgot what she was doing and had to start all over again.

Mr. Helms yelled up the stairs once more.

Just then, Nancy found a right shoe under the bed and stuck it on her mother's foot. Quickly, Jessie found the matching shoe and stuck it on Mrs. Helms's left foot.

"Okay," Mrs. Helms said.

"Wait!" Jessie told her. "Your slip shows."

"Oh, so what!" Mrs. Helms said, but Jessie made her fix it. She loved Mrs. Helms almost as much as her own mother and she wanted her to look nice.

"Aren't you going to wear earrings?" Nancy asked. Mrs. Helms also lost earrings, but she always bought two pairs so that she could lose one and still have two—for a while, anyway.

"Why not wear these?" Jessie said, holding up a pair that Mrs. Helms had once told her were made from porcupine quills. That got them to talking about porcupines, and finally Mr. Helms had to come upstairs and practically drag his wife down the stairs.

"Have fun!" Mrs. Helms called as she went out the front door. "We won't be back too late. Then we'll all go out to dinner." And they were gone.

"I'm hungry right now," Nancy announced.

"Me, too," Jessie said.

They went into the kitchen and began opening all the cabinets. There were cake mixes and cereals and cans of soup, but that wasn't what they wanted at all. Jessie started getting hungrier just from looking at everything. She opened up a box of graham crackers and started nibbling on them. She liked to take little tiny bites and then let it get all mushy in her mouth. It was kind of disgusting, especially if you opened your mouth. But only really gross kids like Gary and Kenny did something like that.

"I've got it!" Nancy yelled.

"What?" Jessie asked, with her mouth full.

"Marshmallows!" Nancy explained, grabbing a bag off the shelf.

"Plain marshmallows?" asked Jessie.

"No. We'll toast them and put them on graham crackers. With chocolate!" Nancy said triumphantly.

"S'mores," Jessie said. "That's a great idea."

"I know," Nancy said modestly.

"But how will we toast them? You don't have a fireplace," Jessie pointed out.

"Yeah," Nancy said, sounding discouraged. "We don't even have a gas stove."

"Let's have something else," Jessie suggested. "Or let's eat them raw."

"No," Nancy said. Sometimes she was very stubborn. "What we need is a fire."

"It's too dark out now," Jessie pointed out, "and anyway it's too cold."

"So we'll build a fire inside," Nancy said.

"But we'll burn down the house," Jessie told her.

"Not if we put it in something," Nancy said.

Jessie looked around the kitchen. "What about the sink?"

Nancy shook her head. "We might clog the drain." Then she started banging open cupboard doors again. "How about this?" She held up a big white pot. It was very old and scratched up. It was perfect.

They ran outside, gathered up sticks and leaves, and threw them in the pot. Then they lit them. In a few seconds it was burning away like a campfire right inside the house.

At first, everything wouldn't melt right. A couple of marshmallows caught fire and fell into the pot. Finally, Jessie figured out a way to hold the sticks high enough over the fire. The s'mores were delicious. They each had about twelve. They were very full.

"Boy, it's really smoky in here," Jessie said, after a while, looking around.

"We'd better air it out," Nancy agreed. She opened the back door. Nothing happened.

"Maybe we should open both doors," Jessie suggested. She ran and opened the front door. That made a big wind, which blew everything around. Papers and magazines went sailing everywhere. But it did get rid of the smoke. Jessie picked up the stuff on the floor and put it into neat piles.

"There. Now you would never know," Nancy said.

"Except for the pot," Jessie reminded her.

"Right." Nancy said. "We'd better scrub it out."

Jessie went over to pick it up. "Yeeowch!" It was really hot. Nancy handed her pot holders and Jessie grabbed it again. She gave it a tug. Then she pulled even harder.

"What is the matter?" asked Nancy.

"It's stuck," Jessie whispered.

"What?"

"It's stuck!" yelled Jessie. "It's stuck in the floor."

"Let me do it." Nancy shoved Jessie out of the way. She pulled on the pot with all her strength. It didn't move.

"Maybe we should try together," suggested Jessie.

They each grabbed one side of the pot and yanked as hard as they could. They tugged and tugged. They pulled so hard they bumped heads. Usually they would have thought that was funny, but this was an emergency.

"What are we going to do?" wailed Nancy. "My mother will kill me."

Jessie thought as hard as she could. "I've got it!"

"What?" asked Nancy.

"Well, it got stuck because the floor melted, right?" Jessie said. "So what we have to do is unmelt it."

Nancy stared at her. "You're crazy."

"No. What we have to do is freeze it," Jessie explained.

"What should we do?" said Nancy. "Put the floor in the freezer?"

"No . . ." Jessie said slowly. "We'll fill up the pot with ice cubes."

"You are a genius!" Nancy shrieked. She ran over to the refrigerator and started practically throwing ice cubes at Jessie. She even threw in some frozen vegetables.

When the pot was almost full they grabbed hold of both sides and yanked. It didn't budge. Jessie couldn't think of anything else to do. She felt like crying.

"Maybe we could stick a knife under it and sort of pry it up," Nancy suggested.

She got a long wood-handled knife and very carefully, so that she wouldn't cut herself, slipped it under the edge of the pot. She bent it up. There was a loud snap, and the end of the knife broke off.

"Ohhh, no!" Now Nancy was the one who looked as though she was about to cry.

Jessie pulled on the pot with every bit of strength she had. It moved. "Help me!" she yelled.

The two of them yanked as hard as they could. There was a big crack. The pot came free. They had done it!

Jessie and Nancy looked down. There was a flat round spot in the linoleum that was lower than the rest of the floor. The point of the knife was stuck in it and it was sort of soft and yucky. They grabbed the broken knife and used it to scrape out the point of the blade. Then they smoothed down the part of the floor that had melted. It was still a little mushy, but at least you could walk on it.

"What do you think?" Jessie said. Now that it was over, she was starting to get a little nervous.

"Oh, it's fine," Nancy said happily.

"But somebody will notice," Jessie pointed out.

"But it's all right. It's just a little . . . lumpy," Nancy reassured her. "I bet they won't even be able to tell."

Jessie wasn't too sure, but there wasn't any time to argue. They could hear the car in the driveway. They hid the pot, quickly washed the knife, threw out the piece of the blade that had broken off, and ran up to Nancy's room.

"Nancy!" They heard Mrs. Helms call from downstairs. "Jessie!"

They looked at each other.

"Maybe she just wants to see if we're here," Nancy said.

"Get down here, you two!" Nancy's mother yelled. "Now!"

Slowly, they went downstairs. Mrs. Helms stood at the kitchen door, glaring at them. Jessie didn't know where to look. Usually when a grownup gets mad, you look down at the floor, but that didn't seem like a very good idea.

"What did you do?" Mrs. Helms asked. "We were

only gone for a couple of hours. How did you manage to ruin the kitchen floor so fast? Breaking things comes naturally to Nancy, but I am surprised at you, Jessica. How could you let Nancy talk you into whatever it was she talked you into?"

Mrs. Helms was yelling. Jessie had never seen her yell before. It was scary.

Nancy started to cry. "That's not fair. You don't know it was my idea."

"It wasn't *my* idea," Jessie said. "You thought it up."

"But you wanted to do it," Nancy said.

"It's your house, Nancy; you know the rules around here. You aren't supposed to destroy floors, for heaven's sake," Mrs. Helms said.

"But why don't you blame her, too?" Nancy cried.

"I am. I'm blaming both of you."

"But you're yelling at me more. And I know why. It's because you think she's so good. Old P. J. never does anything wrong, so you blame me! You're mean."

"Nancy!" Jessie started to cry. "You said you'd never call me that."

Just then Mr. Helms walked into the kitchen. "What is going on here?" Then he saw the floor. "Goodness, how did you do that?" He sounded really curious.

Nancy said very slowly, "I guess it sort of was my idea."

"But I helped," Jessie added.

Then Nancy smiled at her. "I'm sorry I blamed you. Okay?"

"I guess so," Jessie said. Because after all, Nancy *was* her best friend, and when your mother yells at you, you say dumb things. Everybody knows that.

"Well . . ." said Mrs. Helms.

Then Nancy started telling about the marshmallows and the fire. A couple of times Jessie had to help her out because Nancy couldn't remember what happened next. Mr. and Mrs. Helms just stared at them. It made them a little nervous. But when they got to the part about the ice cubes and the frozen vegetables, they heard a little sound. It was Mrs. Helms. She was giggling. She was trying to look very stern, but little laugh sounds were escaping from the corners of her mouth. By the time they described smoothing out the floor, Mr. and Mrs. Helms were laughing out loud.

"Where's the pot?" Mrs. Helms asked. Jessie pulled it out of the closet. It was full of old ashes and melted ice, with some peas and carrots and broccoli floating in it. It was pretty disgusting.

"We'll clean it really well," Jessie offered.

"You sure will," Mrs. Helms said firmly. But at least she wasn't mad any more.

"Jessie," Nancy whispered that night when they were in bed. "Jessie, are you still mad at me?"

Jessie didn't say anything.

"I told them it was my fault," Nancy reminded her.

Jessie still didn't say anything.

"Are you mad because I called you . . . that?" Nancy

finally asked. "I really am sorry and I'll never do it again. I promise."

"But you already promised and then you did it."

"I told you I was sorry. If you are best friends you have to say it's okay."

"And you'll never do it again?" Jessie asked suspiciously.

"Never," Nancy said. "And anyway, you know what?"

"What?"

"I don't think you really *are* perfect."

✎ TWO

"'THE WORLD OF DINOSAURS' IS ON T.V. TONIGHT!" KENNY was whispering so loud practically every kid in the class could hear him.

Dinosaurs were all that he and Gary had been talking about for the past week. If you listened to them you would think that this was the most important program that had ever been on T.V. since it was invented. They had been drawing pictures of tyrannosauruses and stegosauruses and brontosauruses all over their notebooks. They had been stomping all around the cafeteria at lunchtime making weird sounds. They called them dinousaur cries, which was really stupid because nobody knows what dinosaurs sounded like.

"Your attention, please," Mrs. Rogers was saying. "Open your science books to chapter twelve."

"Science," yelled Kenny. "Great."

Mrs. Rogers looked very surprised that Kenny was excited about anything that happened in class. "Have you decided to become a scientist, Kenny?"

"He's decided to become a dinosaur," Nancy whispered to Jessie.

"I want to learn about prehistoric monsters," Kenny explained to Mrs. Rogers.

"But *we* are studying sedimentary formations. Or at least the rest of us are," Mrs. Rogers told him.

"Old rocks," Ben snickered. "That's perfect for Kenny, because he's got rocks for brains."

Mrs. Rogers pretended that she hadn't heard Ben and began the lesson. It was pretty boring. When it was finally over and it was time to give out homework, Kenny and Gary started jumping around in their seats, waving their hands.

"What is it?" Mrs. Rogers asked, before they exploded or knocked over their desks.

Kenny and Gary started talking at the same time, explaining about how wonderful "The World of Dinosaurs" was going to be. The whole time Ben was making weird noises, which he said were dinosaur war cries. It got pretty loud.

"So can't we watch it for homework instead of learning about stupid old rocks?"

Jessie and Nancy looked at each other. Gary was really dumb. You should never tell teachers that homework is stupid. They get very insulted.

"Television is not homework," Mrs. Rogers said firmly.

"But why not?" wailed Kenny.

"Homework is supposed to make you think," Mrs. Rogers explained.

Ben was still making strange noises, even though Mrs. Rogers kept telling him to be quiet.

"Homework is wasted on Kenny," Nancy whispered.

"Yeah, he couldn't think if he tried," Jessie whispered back.

"Since so many of you are interested in dinosaurs," Mrs. Rogers said, looking at Ben, who finally shut up, "maybe you would like to do a special report on the program." Ben smiled, and Gary and Kenny started nodding. "In addition to your regular homework."

Jessie started to giggle and Ben gave her a mean look.

Nancy and Jessie stayed after school for Nature Club. Jessie was working on a picture of birch trees.

They were really hard to do because they had silvery bark and there wasn't any silver paint, just gray, and that's not the same thing at all. It was late by the time they started home.

"Don't walk so fast," Nancy complained. "I'm getting all worn out."

"Okay." Jessie slowed down. "I just don't want to be late for family hour."

"I'm glad we don't have one of those," Nancy said. "But we couldn't because my mother is always late for everything."

"Mine isn't," Jessie said. "She's never late for anything."

"She has to be late sometimes," Nancy said.

"Nope. Never," Jessie said.

"That's too bad," Nancy said. "Of course, sometimes it's good. When you're in a hurry it's terrible having a mother who's late, because people never believe you and they always think it's your fault. Especially teachers."

"I guess so," Jessie agreed.

"Can I borrow your science homework tomorrow?" Nancy asked.

"No!" Jessie said. "You're supposed to do your own homework."

"I know, but we have so much, and I want to watch 'The World of Dinosaurs.' I'll never get it done, and Mrs. Rogers will yell at me again."

"But I want to watch it too!" Jessie said.

"How can you? Your parents make you do your homework before T.V."

"So?" Jessie said. "Maybe I'll just say we didn't have any tonight."

"But they'll never believe you. We always have homework," Nancy pointed out.

"What are you going to do?" Jessie asked.

"I was going to copy yours. But if you don't do any, I'll have to get up early and do it then," Nancy said. "And I'll probably get it all wrong and of course it will be all sloppy . . ."

"So maybe I'll do mine in the morning and it will be all sloppy too," Jessie told her.

"Jessie, your homework is never sloppy," Nancy laughed. "It's always . . ." Then she realized what she was about to say and she stopped.

"I love dinosaurs and I want to learn about them!" Jessie said. "And anyway, everybody else will watch and if I don't they'll all make fun of me."

"Who cares? My mother always says that you have to ignore people and do what you want."

"But what I want to do is watch T.V. Your mother lets you do that and so does everybody else's mother."

"But you can still do your homework and nobody will ever know," Nancy went on. "I'll tell you all about the program in the morning . . . while I'm copying your homework."

"NO!" Jessie shouted. "It's wrong to copy home-work, and besides, I'm not even going to do it. I don't care what my parents say—or anybody else."

Nancy looked really surprised, but she didn't say a word.

By the time family hour was over and they had eaten dinner, there was only a half-hour left until the dinosaur program. Jessie opened her notebook and wrote as fast as she could. She made a mistake in the middle of the second problem and tried to erase it. It made a big hole in the paper. She looked at the clock. Only seven minutes left. She would never finish in time. Two minutes left to go. She stared down at the paper. Then she shut her notebook and went downstairs.

"Did you finish already?" her mother asked in surprise.

"Yes," Jessie said, being very careful not to look at her.

"What are you doing down here so early?" her father asked. He came into the living room with his newspaper open to the crossword puzzle.

"We had hardly any homework tonight," she explained quickly. "That's because there's a very educational program on T.V. about dinosaurs."

"Really?" said her father. "I love dinosaurs." He turned on the T.V. and sat down to watch it with her.

It was the most excellent program that Jessie had ever seen, even if it wasn't funny. It was too bad that dinosaurs were extinct because they were really interesting and she would love to see a real one.

Her parents liked the show, too. She could tell

because her mother kept nodding at the T.V. and her father made little *harrumph* sounds in the back of his throat, which is what he always did when he thought something was interesting.

When the program was over, her mother kissed her good night.

"It's time for bed, Jess," she said.

"Good night, Jessico," her father said, giving her a hug.

"Good night," Jessie said, hugging him back.

When she got to her room she looked at her notebooks again. Then she picked them up, went into the closet, and shut the door behind her. She crouched down under the clothes and by the closet light she finished her homework. It wasn't quite as neat as usual but it was almost all finished when she heard her parents coming to bed.

Jessica quickly put her books back on the desk and just got into bed before the door opened. Her mother came in to check on her. She peeked out from under her eyelashes and saw her mother turn off the closet light and shut the door. She was safe. She rolled over and fell right to sleep. After all, it was way past her bedtime.

The next morning Jessica got to her homeroom a second before the bell rang. She had slept right through her alarm and her mother had to shake her to get her out of bed.

She sat down, opened up her notebook, and took out her homework. It looked awful. The handwriting slanted all over the page, and it was full of smudges. She had never handed in work like this before. But at least she had seen the program.

Mrs. Rogers was already beginning to collect homework from the row of desks right next to Jessie's. For a second, Jessica thought about putting it back into her book. But it was too late. Mrs. Rogers was standing right in front of her row. The kids in back of her began passing their papers up to the front of the room. It was Jessica's turn. She couldn't move. Her hands felt frozen. Nancy turned around to see what was holding everything up. Mrs. Rogers looked at her impatiently.

"Jessica, I'd like to get on with the day's work."

Jessica made her arms move. She picked up the messy paper and handed it in. Nancy gave her a funny look, then she put her homework on top of Jessica's and put her book report, which still had a footprint on the first page, on top of the whole pile. Jessie kept her head down so she wouldn't have to look at Mrs. Rogers.

At lunchtime Nancy grabbed Jessie. "Did you really watch?"

"Yup," Jessie said.

"What did your parents say?" Nancy asked, with her mouth full.

"They understood . . . sort of," Jessie said. She didn't want to talk about it, but Nancy kept on asking questions.

"Did you do your homework?"

"Yeah," Jessie answered. "I just stayed up real late."

"Did you get it right?" Nancy demanded.

"Sure," Jessie said.

"Wow." Nancy was impressed. "I don't think mine was. I wish I could have checked your answers, but Mrs. Rogers was standing right over me. There wasn't even time to sneak a peek."

"Hey! That rhymes!" shouted Jessie, trying to change the subject.

They tried saying "sneak a peek" ten times, as fast as they could. They only got through nine before they started laughing too hard to finish.

After school Jessie told the other kids that she couldn't play kickball bcecause she had to go to the dentist.

"I bet it will really hurt," Ben said.

"Yeah. Cavities are terrible," Kenny said.

"Jessie never gets cavities," Nancy bragged.

"Of course not," Ben said. "She has perfect teeth, and the dentist loves her. He probably gives her a balloon for brushing her teeth so much. She's the dentist's pet, too. Maybe he even gives her one of those big teeth they have in the office."

"I do too get cavities," Jessie protested. "I get lots."

"Oh, yeah?" Gary said. "How many?"

"Two," Jessie said.

"That's nothing," Kenny bragged. "I get three every time I go to the dentist."

"I never even go to the dentist," Ben snickered. "My mother doesn't even make me go anymore because the last time I went I bit the dentist. Hard."

All the boys laughed. Jessie wished she really was going to the dentist and that she had twenty cavities. But her mother wouldn't let her eat sugar, and anyway she had very strong teeth. She left the rest of them choosing up teams for kickball and went home.

She sat down at her desk. She was never going to turn in terrible homework again.

Jessie decided to start with science. That was usually the hardest. She added diagrams to show how well she understood the lesson. She heard the door open downstairs. Her parents were home and it was time for family hour.

Her mother looked at her, surprised. "I didn't know you were home already!"

"I had a lot of homework," she explained.

"I'm surprised at Mrs. Rogers," her father said. "Yesterday you had almost no homework and today you have so much you don't have time to play after school. This does not encourage good study habits."

"Nobody was playing today anyhow," Jessie said quickly. "Gary and Kenny had to go to the dentist."

"Let's drop the subject," her mother said firmly. "This isn't the time for this discussion. Dentists upset me." Sometimes Jessica was glad there were so many rules about family hour.

She could hardly wait for dinner to be over so she could go back and finish her science drawings. She colored the sandstone in burnt orange and the limestone in lilac. It looked beautiful. Then she cut out pictures from a magazine for her social studies work and put it in a cover that she made out of construction paper.

By the time she was finished it was after nine o'clock. There wouldn't be any time for television tonight. But she didn't care. There weren't any good programs on and her homework was really beautiful. In fact, it was probably the best she had ever done.

When she got her messy homework back the next day she couldn't even look at it. She didn't want to know what Mrs. Rogers had written on it.

Finally, when everyone else had gone off to lunch and the room was empty, she turned it over. There was nothing written on it. Not a word. Then she saw in the corner Mrs. Rogers had written the word *Correct*, just the way she always did. Maybe Mrs. Rogers somehow knew that she had done wonderful homework to make up for this.

✎ THREE

"HURRY UP, JESSIE," NANCY WAS CALLING.

For a minute Jessie didn't know what Nancy was talking about. Then she remembered. Today was the first meeting of the Summer Drama Society. Today they would find out what play they would perform in Town Hall Auditorium this August. Nancy was tugging at her, dragging her toward the school parking lot.

"Stop pulling me!" she said to Nancy.

"I want to get there early," Nancy explained.

"But you know that your mom will be late picking us up. She's always late."

"You're right," Nancy said cheerfully. "I think sometimes she forgets where she's going and goes someplace else instead. Then she has to turn around and start over."

Nancy's mother fooled them. She was waiting in the parking lot. But she did take a couple of wrong streets, and by the time they got there the meeting was almost ready to start.

Mrs. Helms got out of the car with them.

"Are you going to try out?" Jessica asked Mrs. Helms as they walked into the auditorium.

"Oh, no!" Nancy's mom said, and she blushed a little bit. There weren't many moms who would blush in front of their own kids.

Jessie looked around. It looked as though almost everyone in town wanted to be in the play this year. Of course they weren't all going to be actors. There would be scenery to build, and an orchestra and a stage crew.

"Look," Nancy tugged at Jessica.

"That's Jim," Jessie explained to Mrs. Helms, pointing to a very good-looking blond guy. "He's in charge of the lights and stuff like that."

"He goes crawling around in the ceiling and practically hangs from those pipes up there," Nancy told her mother.

"We watched him last year," Jessie added. They didn't tell Mrs. Helms that last summer they had decided that Jim was the best-looking boy they had ever seen, except for actors on T.V.

Then a couple of junior high school kids who had been in the chorus last year with Jessie and Nancy came over to say hello. Jessie and Nancy smiled at each other. They really felt they belonged.

Just then, Miss Shaw, who always directed the plays, came in and stood at the front of the hall. Everyone quieted down to hear her. She announced the name of the play they were going to do. Jessie had never heard of it, but Mrs. Helms whispered that they would go to the bookstore after the meeting and buy copies.

Miss Shaw started to introduce everybody, but Jessica was getting too excited to listen. She wanted the meeting to be over so they could buy the scripts. She wanted to go home and read it and play all the parts by herself.

By the time the meeting was over, the bookstore was closed. Mrs. Helms promised she would get them the playscripts the next day.

"I'm going to try out for a part this year," Nancy announced as they drove home.

"Me, too," Jessie said. "Not a big part or anything like that."

"Yeah, because the older kids get all the good stuff," Nancy complained.

"Don't worry," Mrs. Helms told her. "I promise that

someday you will be one of the older kids."

"Oh, Mom."

"You passed my house," Jessie reminded Mrs. Helms.

The next day Jessie and Nancy talked about the play all the way to school. It wasn't until the bell rang and they had to be quiet that Jessie remembered that today was the day she would get back her wonderful homework.

Her heart was thumping when she took it from Mrs. Rogers. She turned it over. There was nothing written on her fantastic homework. Maybe the top page had gotten lost. She hoped Mrs. Rogers hadn't kept it to show the class. That would be terrible. Ben would call her teacher's pet again and everybody would tease her.

She looked at her paper again. Then she saw, written in the corner, one word—*Correct*. Mrs. Rogers couldn't tell great homework from terrible homework. Or else she never read it at all. She hadn't wanted Mrs. Rogers to tell the other kids how good her work was, but she did want Mrs. Rogers to know. She had done all that extra work to show that she knew homework was supposed to make you think, and Mrs. Rogers didn't even care. The other kids had known that all the time; that was why they didn't care if their homework was right or not. She was the only stupid person in the whole fifth grade who did extra homework instead of watching T.V.

"I scored two runs today in kickball," she told her father.

"Jessie, that's great!" he said. "Did anything else happen in school today?"

She thought about that for a minute. She couldn't tell her parents that Mrs. Rogers didn't read the homework, because they wouldn't have believed her. Teachers were supposed to read assignments, and her parents thought that everybody did what they were supposed to do. That was because *they* always did. They would think Jessie was complaining if she told them what had happened, and you weren't supposed to complain during family hour; you were supposed to share. She didn't want to share the part about not doing her homework the night of "The World of Dinosaurs." So there was nothing she could say.

"Jessie!" Nancy was standing outside Jessie's door, shouting. "Hurry up! I've got them." In her hand were two little soft-covered books—the playscripts.

Jessie took one and opened it. It smelled brand-new. As they walked to school, Nancy told her the whole story. She had stayed up practically all night reading it.

Then they started acting out all the parts. They decided that they were both truly great.

Gary and Kenny were already hanging out in front of school when Jessie and Nancy got there. They started giggling and pointing at Jessie.

"Here comes P.J.," Gary yelled.

"You mean T.P.," Ben said.

"T.P. for toilet paper," Kenny yelled.

"Don't pay any attention," Nancy whispered.

"Nooooo," Ben said. "T.P. for teacher's pet and *also* for toilet paper."

"You guys are so stupid and so ugly that you make the whole school nauseous!" Nancy shouted.

"Look who's talking," Ben said. "The girl with the scabbiest knees in the fifth grade."

"Teacher's pet's best friend," added Kenny.

"I am not the teacher's pet," Jessie screamed as loud as she could.

"Oh, yeah?" said Ben. "Prove it."

"Okay, I will. I hate Mrs. Rogers," Jessie said. "I hate her more than anything."

"Jessie!" Nancy said. "She's better than Mrs. Grimes, and we were almost in her class, remember."

"Let's see how much you hate her," Kenny sneered.

"I dare you to do something to get her mad," Gary added.

"Okay," Jessie said. "I will."

Then the bell rang. As they were walking into class, Nancy whispered to Jessie, "I told you to ignore them. Why should you get into trouble to make them happy? They don't deserve it."

"You don't understand anything," Jessie whispered back.

Nancy looked hurt, but Jessie didn't care. Anything was better than being the teacher's pet, especially since Mrs. Rogers didn't deserve to have a pet.

Mrs. Rogers started collecting homework. Jessie's

hands were trembling and her stomach felt funny. Not exactly bad, just strange. The kid in the back of the row passed up his homework and everybody put theirs on top until it came to Jessica.

"Jessica," Mrs. Rogers said.

"I don't have mine," Jessica murmured.

Everyone turned around. Her heart was beating very fast.

"Why not?"

"My dog wet on it," Jessica explained. Mrs. Rogers looked surprised. Jessie was, too. She didn't even have a dog. She didn't know what made her say that. It got very quiet. Then the kids began to giggle.

"It got all yellow and soggy so I couldn't bring it in," she explained. The other kids laughed harder. "And it smelled," she went on.

"That's quite enough, Jessica," Mrs. Rogers said. "Quiet down, class, and open your science books. Jessica, I will talk to you later."

While everyone was getting out their books, Nancy turned around to look at her. Nancy knew Jessie's mother was allergic to dogs.

For the whole rest of the morning Jessie wondered what Mrs. Rogers would do to her. She hoped it wouldn't be too terrible. But at least she wasn't the teacher's pet anymore.

When all the other kids left for lunch, Mrs. Rogers called her back. "Jessie, I'll excuse you this time for not having your homework, because I know it isn't like you.

But don't let it happen again. All right?"

Jessica nodded, even though she didn't think it was all right at all.

"You can go have lunch now," Mrs. Rogers told her. "But I think this afternoon after school you should begin to housebreak your dog."

Jessica wondered why Mrs. Rogers said that.

The other kids were all waiting for her when she got to the cafeteria.

"What did she do to you?" Nancy asked.

"Do you have detention?" demanded Gary.

"Or did she kiss you and hug you and tell you never to be bad again?" Ben said.

"She said I had to do my homework," Jessie told him. "Twice."

"The same thing twice?" Nancy asked. "Why?"

Jessie just shrugged and sat down to eat.

Patty, the girl who sat across the aisle from Jessica, came over to her. "Do you really have a dog?"

All the other kids got quiet. "Nope," Jessie said.

"You made up all that stuff?" Kenny asked, sounding surprised.

"Yup," Jessie said.

"It was pretty funny," Patty said, and she went and got in line for more milk.

✎ FOUR

THAT WEEKEND JESSIE WENT WITH HER PARENTS TO HER grandmother's house. Every two months the whole family had dinner together. It was like family hour, only bigger. Sometimes there were almost forty people. All her cousins came. Her first cousins and her second cousins and her aunts and uncles and her great-aunt and her great-uncle. The trouble was that the two cousins who were closest to her in age were boys, Billy and Charley.

Billy and Charley were terrible. Not as bad as Ben, but almost.

Once Jessie had to sit between them at dinner. It was the worst meal ever. The two of them kept leaning behind her and knocking each other's heads and yelling "nuggie." Then they had a food fight. Jessica had to dive under the table so she wouldn't get mashed potatoes all over her dress. Still, they always seemed to have more fun than Jessie.

Everyone was saying hello and hugging and asking her how school was. Out of the corner of her eye Jessica saw Billy and Charley sneaking out of the living room. She had to find out what they were up to. Luckily, just then her cousin Sandy came in with her new baby, William. While everyone was crowding around the baby, Jessica escaped into the hallway.

There they were, crouched under the stairs, whispering. She went over and crouched next to them.

"What are you doing here?" Billy asked.

"Yeah. Why aren't you in the living room getting your cheek pinched?" Charley teased. It was true. For some reason a lot of people in the family pinched Jessica's cheek. She didn't know why and she hated it.

"What are you doing?" she asked.

"None of your business," Charley told her.

"Come on, what are you doing?" she asked again.

"Why do you want to know, P.J.?" Billy asked.

"Don't call me that," Jessica yelled.

"Shhhhhhhhh!" they both said, sticking their hands

over her mouth. "Do you want Grandma to come out here?"

"Yeah, then we'll get in trouble for being mean to you," Billy said.

"And we didn't want you to come out here in the first place," Charley whispered loudly.

She bit Billy's hand. He pulled it away as fast as he could.

"See?" Jessica grinned. "I am not Perfect Jessica." This time she remembered to whisper.

"Oh yeah?" Charley said. "You never get in trouble!"

Billy was still holding on to the hand Jessie bit. "P.J., P.J., P.J.," he whispered.

"I am not," Jessica hissed.

"Name one bad thing you did," Billy said.

"I told the teacher that my dog wet on my homework," Jessica bragged.

"That's nothing," Billy shrugged.

"We don't even have a dog," Jessica reminded them.

"Is that the worst thing you ever did?" Charley sounded amazed.

"Come on." Billy dragged Charley to his feet. "Let's go."

"Where are you going?" Jessie demanded.

"We aren't telling," said Billy. And the two of them ran out the back door.

Jessica went back into the living room. Her aunt Amy was telling everyone about her baby, Brad. He was two years old. Brad had gotten into the bathroom and then unscrewed the door knob and locked himself in. They had to call the super to take down the whole door to get him out. Everyone laughed and Brad looked very proud of himself.

"He's a handful," her grandmother said.

"At least," Aunt Amy agreed.

"Different from Jessica, that's for sure," her grandmother said.

Her mother smiled at her. "The best baby in the world."

"You were such a pretty baby," her grandmother told her.

Jessie ducked before her grandmother could pinch her cheek.

Friday was Jessica's favorite day of the week because that was when they had art class. Mrs. Goodwyn came into their classroom pushing her big wooden cart full of supplies. All the other kids said that Mrs. Goodwyn was crazy, but she really wasn't. They just said that because she had purple hair. It wasn't really purple, it was more like violet, and it was very pretty. Jessie and Nancy had decided that when they were older they were going to dye their hair purple, too. They told that to Mrs. Helms, but she told them that purple might be out of fashion when they were old enough to change their hair color. Jessie didn't care. Even if it was old-fashioned she was going to have purple hair.

This month they weren't painting; they were making

rugs. You had to tie about a million little pieces of yarn to string and when you were finally done, you had a real rug. A little one, but it was still a rug.

Jessie's was really beautiful. It had purple in it (in honor of Mrs. Goodwyn's hair), and pink and orange and red. Mrs. Goodwyn came over to look at it. "Jessica, that is a work of art. An original and very creative project. You can cut it off the loom now and tie on fringe. I'll show you how."

She took out a pair of scissors and snipped away. "Look, class. This is what a rya rug is supposed to look like. The rest of you could be finished too if you had worked as hard as Jessica." Then she held up the rug for everyone to see.

"It's ugly," Ben said.

"Ben, you have the taste and artistic sensibility of a snail," Mrs. Goodwyn told him. She didn't like Ben very much and she didn't pretend that she did. That was very unusual in a teacher, and one of the reasons that Jessie liked her so much. It was also one of the reasons that Ben didn't.

Mrs. Goodwyn left Jessie a ball of string to make fringe with, gathered everything up on her cart, and wheeled it away. They were still supposed to have ten more minutes of art class, but Mrs. Goodwyn left early. She said she had more important things to do.

"Look at old P.J." Ben said. "She's a double T.P."

"She's everybody's little pet," Gary agreed. Mrs. Goodwyn had said that a monkey could make a nicer rya rug than he had.

"Come here, little pet," Ben said, snapping his fingers.

Jessie tried very hard to look at her rug and ignore them.

"Let's see you do some of your little pet tricks," Kenny giggled.

"Roll over, little pet," Ben commanded. "Sit up and beg and you can have a nice doggy biscuit and no more homework."

Jessie didn't look up.

"Let's see the perfect rya rug," Ben said, coming over to Jessica's desk. He reached for it, but Jessie grabbed it tightly.

"NO!" she said.

"Leave her alone," Nancy told the boys.

"Shut up." Kenny shoved Nancy, and Ben grabbed Jessie's art project.

"Give it back," Jessie shouted.

"Catch," Ben said, throwing it to Gary.

Jessie ran over to Gary but he threw it high into the air. "Keep away!" he yelled.

Jessie tried to grab it, but Ben shoved her out of the way and caught it. Jessie started screaming at Ben and she kicked him hard in the shins.

"Oww!" Ben jumped up and down, but he didn't drop the rug.

"Give it back," Jessie said, pulling at him.

"I think this rug needs a shave," Ben said, holding it over her head.

Jessie tried to snatch it back, but Kenny grabbed her arms from behind.

"Let her go!" Nancy yelled. "You can't hit girls."

"She started it," Ben said.

"Just give me back my rug." Jessie pulled away from Kenny and lunged at Ben again. He was a lot taller than she and he waved the rug in the air over her head.

"P.J., P.J., P.J.," Ben kept jeering. "Crying about her ugly rug!"

Ben was tearing at her rug, and pieces of yarn fell onto the floor.

Jessie screamed at Ben again, and she didn't even know what she was saying this time. She started bashing at his chest and neck and tugging on his arms. She threw her whole body against him as hard as she could. She knocked him backward and he fell down. She grabbed back her rug and kicked at him.

She felt arms pulling her away from Ben. She heard Mrs. Rogers yelling at her, shouting her name. "Jessica! What is going on here?"

"He started it," Jessica sobbed. "He was going to tear up my rug."

"Get back to your seats, both of you," Mrs. Rogers ordered.

Jessica and Ben stood and glared at each other.

"Did you hear me?" Mrs. Rogers demanded. "Sit down." She gave Jessica a shake.

Slowly Jessica walked back to her desk. Her face felt hot and her arms and legs were all trembly. She had never hit anybody like that before. Kids with brothers or sisters had told her how they beat up on each other all the time, but Jessie was the only child in her family, so she had never done that. Kids fought on the playground sometimes, but she had never done that either. She was surprised to discover how strong she was. Maybe she was growing muscles.

When the last bell rang and everybody got ready to go, Mrs. Rogers stopped them.

"I am shocked at your behavior today. Not just Jessica and Ben but the whole class. You could hear the noise all the way down the hall. You are all old enough to be left alone in a classroom for ten minutes without acting like animals or infants." Nobody said anything. "Everyone except Jessica and Ben may leave now, and I hope nothing like this ever happens in this room again."

All the kids gathered up their books very quietly and left. Nancy turned around to Jessica and squeezed her shoulder very quickly, then left with the others. Ben and Jessie sat in the empty classroom and waited for Mrs. Rogers to say something.

The teacher sat down at her desk and wrote on a piece of paper. Then she folded it up and took another sheet of paper, wrote on it and folded that one up, too. She looked up.

"What happened?" she asked.

"She started it," Ben said. "She kicked me."

"Liar!" Jessie shouted.

"Jessica!" Mrs. Rogers said. "Control yourself."

"He took my rya rug. He started to tear it up," Jessie said more quietly.

"That is still no reason to get involved in a brawl," Mrs. Rogers said.

"But I worked on it for a month," Jessica said.

"Ben." Mrs. Rogers gestured for him to come over to her desk. "Here is a note for your parents. I want it returned, signed by both of them, on Monday. You may go now."

After he had gone, Mrs. Rogers turned to Jessie. "I don't understand what has gotten into you, Jessica. You know better than to get into fist fights! You should have come to me, or to another teacher, and we would have saved your art project."

Jessie stared at Mrs. Rogers. She had always thought that Mrs. Rogers was smart, but suddenly she realized that wasn't true. Ben would have ruined her rug before any teacher could have stopped him. And anyway, only a real teacher's pet would have tattled. Even if they had saved her rug, all the other kids would have teased her so much she probably would have had to quit school.

"I have a note for your parents, too," Mrs. Rogers said. "I think they should know what has been going on."

"But that's not fair. He started it."

"But you certainly continued it."

"But why should I get a note when it wasn't my fault?" Jessie protested.

"I am not going to argue about this with you. Take this note, give it to your parents, and bring it back on Monday. Do you understand me?" Mrs. Rogers said sternly.

Jessica nodded. She was too mad to talk. She picked up her books, walked out the door, and went into the girls' room to read the note.

> *Dear Mr. & Mrs. Fowler:*
>
> *Until recently, Jessica has been a model student, but her behavior and her attitude seem to have changed in the last few weeks. There have been a number of minor incidents that have concerned me, but today she permitted herself to be drawn into a fist fight with another student. This is not the Jessica that I am accustomed to seeing, and I am sure you will share my concern. Please feel free to contact me to discuss her behavior.*
>
> *Sincerely, Bernice Rogers*

She read the note a second time and then a third time. She had never had to bring a note home before. She had never had bad behavior before. It wasn't fair.

Everybody always says that you can't let people push you around and she had only been protecting her rya rug. She shouldn't get a note for that. She hoped that her parents would understand, but she didn't think they would. They thought bringing a note home from school was the worst thing that could happen to you. But they were wrong.

✎ FIVE

"JESSIE," HER MOTHER WAS CALLING, "ARE YOU UP?"

Jessie lay in her bed. She knew something awful had happened but she couldn't remember what. She was still too sleepy. Maybe she was having a bad dream.

"Mrs. Helms and Nancy are here. It's time to go to the auditions," her mother yelled.

She woke up. She had to. Then she remembered the

note. It wasn't a dream. It had really happened.

"Jessie, what's the matter?" Her mother was in the doorway. What if she saw the note!

"Nothing. I'll be ready in a minute," Jessie said, jumping out of bed and starting to get dressed.

She went out to the car. The sun was so bright it hurt her eyes.

Mrs. Helms was walking around the car, trying to figure out if one of the tires was flat. "The car seems to tilt," she explained to Jessie.

Jessie got in beside Nancy.

"What happened?" Nancy whispered. "What did Mrs. Rogers do to you?"

"She yelled at me a lot," Jessie said slowly.

"I'm glad that's all," Nancy sighed. "I was really worried that you would get into trouble. Yelling is nothing. That happens to everybody, but if it had been worse . . ."

"Yeah," Jessie said quietly.

"So now everything can go back to being normal," Nancy said happily. "That's the way I like it best."

"Me too," Jessie said softly.

Mrs. Helms got back into the car. "I guess it's all right. All the tires look the same to me." Then she turned to Jessie. "Are you excited about the auditions?"

"I've decided to try out for three parts," Nancy interrupted. "What are you trying out for?"

"I guess I'll just be in the chorus," she said.

"Oh, Jessie, it'll be fun to try out," said Mrs. Helms.

"Yeah," said Nancy. "Who cares if we get a part?"

Jessie wished everyone would stop telling her how to have fun.

When they got to Town Hall Auditorium Nancy jumped out of the car almost before it stopped.

Mrs. Helms turned to Jessica. "Why don't you keep me company while I park the car? Nancy can sign up for both of you."

"Okay," Nancy said, before Jessie could say a word. "See you inside."

Mrs. Helms started to drive around the block, looking for a space.

"Last night Nancy read the whole play to us, acting out all the parts and singing all the songs. She is my own child and I love her dearly but she is completely tone deaf." Nancy's mother laughed and avoided hitting a parking meter by about three inches.

"There's a good place," Jessie said, pointing to an enormous parking spot. That would give Mrs. Helms more room to maneuver. She wasn't very good at parking.

"Can I ask you something, Jessie?" Mrs. Helms gave Jessie a friendly look and backed into a large gray station wagon.

Jessie knew she had to say something or Nancy's mother would wreck the car.

"Okay."

"It's very personal and very important," Mrs. Helms explained seriously.

Jessie stared at her. How could Mrs. Helms have

guessed about the note? She hadn't told anyone.

Mrs. Helms reached into her handbag and turned away from Jessie. When she turned back she was wearing a pair of slightly dusty eyeglasses. "What do you think?" she asked.

Jessie burst out laughing. She didn't mean to, but Mrs. Helms looked so funny, like an owl in a cartoon.

"That bad?" Mrs. Helms asked.

"Oh, no," Jessie reassured her. "They make you look like a real professor."

Mrs. Helms looked happier. "Are you sure?" she asked, looking in the mirror.

"Positive."

"I've been afraid to show anybody. You won't tell anyone how silly I was about them, will you?" Mrs. Helms asked. "Not even Nancy?"

"I promise," Jessie said, getting out of the car.

Mrs. Helms stuck her head out of the window. "Thank you, Jessie. If you ever want to tell me anything, I promise I won't tell anyone else either."

Jessie turned to wave good-bye to Nancy's mom, but all she could see was the sun reflecting from Mrs. Helms's new glasses.

"Hurry up, hurry up!" Nancy was tugging at Jessie. "I signed you up for three parts. I knew you didn't really mean it about just wanting to be in the chorus."

"But . . ." Jessie began. Nancy wasn't listening. She was dragging her down the hall.

"Don't be a chicken," Nancy hissed.

First they had to show that they could sing and dance. They started with the dancing. They were lined up according to height, and Jessie managed to get right behind Nancy. Nancy was the best dancer in Carver Elementary and Jessica figured that if she followed Nancy exactly she would be all right. Nancy grinned at her because she knew what she was doing. Best friends always do.

Mr. Graham showed them their steps. He showed them three times, shouting out numbers while they practiced. Jessica got confused immediately.

"One, two, three, four, and jump," Mr. Graham shouted. About five people jumped late. You could hear their feet after everyone else had stopped. The whole group laughed and they tried it again.

"Start with the other leg," Nancy whispered to Jessica, and pinched her to show which leg to begin with. This time she got it right. Mr. Graham looked at both of them when he said, "Very good." He even seemed surprised.

When they got to the complicated stuff, Jessie had more trouble, even though she tried to make her feet do exactly what Nancy's were doing. But Mr. Graham didn't seem to expect them to be able to do it — hardly anyone could. Jessica was very proud of Nancy. She was almost the best in the whole group.

When they got to the singing part Nancy stood right behind Jessica. Mr. Rhimsky handed out the words to the first song and sang it for them a few times. People sang along in little bits, trying to learn it.

"Now all together," Mr. Rhimsky shouted. And the whole group began to sing. Jessie could hear Nancy howling into her ear. Mrs. Helms was right. Nancy was tone deaf. Mr. Rhimsky was walking down the row listening to everyone.

"Softer," Jessie whispered.

"What?" bellowed Nancy.

"Sing softly."

Nancy looked surprised, but she quieted down. By the time Mr. Rhimsky got to them she was just moving her lips. Jessie made as much noise as she could to make it sound as though they were both singing. Mr. Rhimsky gave them a funny look but he just nodded and moved on.

Then came the acting auditions. A woman walked into the room. She was carrying a large clipboard, which she used to push her glasses up on her nose. She read a list of names. "And Nancy Helms and Jessica Fowler."

The girls followed her down the hall to a huge room with no furniture. It was full of bigger kids. Nancy and Jessie were the only fifth-graders.

Miss Shaw, the director, came in and waited for them to get quiet. She had a very soft, very beautiful voice. Some people said she had once been a professional actress in New York.

"I wanted to speak especially to you younger people. There are a lot of small parts in this show. I'd like you to play them."

Jessie couldn't believe her ears. She had a part. She looked at Nancy. She was really glad that Nancy had signed her up. She was lucky to have such a good friend.

Miss Shaw was still speaking. "Instead of auditions, why don't we do something interesting, so I can get to know you better?"

Then she asked them to do a lot of silly things. Jessie couldn't see what it had to do with being in a play. They were supposed to pick an animal and act it out.

Jessie decided to be a chicken, because Nancy was right — she had almost acted like one. She scratched around on the carpet, clucking and looking for pretend food. She was thinking about laying an egg when she noticed Nancy, who was being a fox, sneaking around right next to her hen house. She squawked as loud as she could, but Nancy the fox just ignored her and started to steal her eggs.

Jessica was very excited by now. She started to peck at Nancy with her beak. She wished there were more chickens to join in with her. They could have made more noise. Then, just as Nancy the fox started to chew her up, a seventh-grader, who was a dog, snarled at Nancy and grabbed her pants cuff. He grabbed so hard that Nancy fell over, practically right on her face. They were all laughing so much by the end that they could hardly breathe. Even Miss Shaw joined in.

Mrs. Helms was waiting for them outside after the auditions.

"What are those?" Nancy asked, pointing at her mother's nose.

"What are what?" Mrs. Helms asked innocently. Jessie giggled.

"Those glasses," Nancy said.

"Oh. Well, you remember that I went to see Doctor Marshall?" Nancy's mother began.

"But that was about a month ago," Nancy exclaimed.

"It was not. Only three weeks ago yesterday," her mother pointed out.

"And he gave you glasses?" Nancy asked.

"He said I was nearsighted," her mother explained.

"So that's why you bump into things a lot," Nancy said. "But why don't you ever wear them?"

"I thought they looked funny," Mrs. Helms confessed.

"You hit the garage twice last week," Nancy scolded her mother.

"It was an accident!"

"Anyway," Nancy said, studying her mother. "You look kind of cute."

Mrs. Helms turned and winked at Jessica.

Jessie didn't want the afternoon to end. She didn't want to leave them. But they were turning on to Jessica's street. She watched as they drove off, then very slowly went into her house.

Jessica's parents were hurrying to get dressed for a party.

"I'm glad you're back," her mother said. "I made dinner for you and it's in the refrigerator. Don't stay up all night watching television. The number is next to the kitchen phone if you need us." Her mother only had on half her makeup and her face looked funny.

"Hi," her father said, trying to choose a tie. "Which one do you like, Jessie?"

"Not that one," she said pointing at a maroon tie. "It looks like it has bugs on it."

"Those aren't bugs," her father said, examining the tie. "They're blobs."

"How did you do at your auditions, Jessica?" her mother asked.

"She did brilliantly, of course," her father said, giving her a kiss. There wasn't enough time to tell them about being animals or anything else. They were certainly in too big a hurry to try and talk to them about notes. That would take a long time. She would have to wait until tomorrow. She didn't want to make her parents late. Her father hated not being on time.

On Sundays, family hour was in the afternoon. All morning Jessica watched the clock, trying to make the hands slow down so she would never have to tell. Her parents must have come home very late last night because they slept all morning. Jessie was very quiet. She didn't want to wake them up. Maybe they would sleep all day.

"Jessica!" her mother called. "What are you doing?"

Slowly she went to join them. Her father was pouring himself another cup of coffee. He still looked sleepy.

Maybe she should wait until he really woke up.

"You never really told us about the auditions," her mother said. She was cutting the buttons off an old jacket and dropping them into the button box. When she was little, Jessie used to play with the buttons. She wished she was that little now, still in nursery school, where you couldn't do anything wrong.

"When are they going to say what part you got?" her father asked.

"In a couple of weeks," Jessie mumbled.

"Why are you mumbling, Jessica?" her mother asked. "Didn't you get enough sleep?"

"How was the party?" Jessica asked. She wanted to change the subject. She had not been able to sleep for a minute last night. How could anybody who had gotten a note from the teacher sleep?

"It was okay," her mother answered.

"Mom" — Jessie took a deep breath.

Her father interrupted her, chuckling. "Do you know Ben Carney?" he asked.

She looked up. How could her parents know about Ben? Maybe they knew about her fight, too.

"His parents were there last night." Her mother shook her head. "Celia used to be such a lovely looking woman."

"She was," her father agreed. "But having a kid like Ben is enough to make anyone old before their time."

Jessica was amazed. But it made sense. Worrying about a bad child *could* make a parent old.

"Well, Bob and Celia shouldn't blame themselves," her mother said, cutting off another button.

"It's true. Some kids are just born wild. There isn't anything you can do," her father said.

"We were lucky," her mother said, smiling at Jessica.

Jessica tried to smile back. How could she tell them about the note?

That night after she had brushed her teeth twice, washed her face, and kissed her parents good night, she went into her room and shut the door.

Jessie opened her closet, crouched on the floor, and took out Mrs. Rogers's note. She picked up a ball-point pen, like the ones her father used. For a minute she hesitated, then she took a deep breath and wrote her father's initials on the note. She inspected it very carefully. She had done a perfect job.

Monday morning was beautiful. Jessie left her house early and waited for Nancy. It was so warm they didn't even need their jackets. Everyone was early, so they played statues in the school yard until the bell rang.

Jessica passed in her homework with the rest of the class. Everything was perfectly normal. Maybe Mrs. Rogers had forgotten about the note.

But as they were leaving for lunch, Mrs. Rogers called her back.

"Did you give your parents my note?" she asked.

Jessie nodded.

"May I have it, please?"

Slowly she handed over the note. Mrs. Rogers opened it and Jessica held her breath.

Mrs. Rogers looked surprised. Suddenly Jessie wished that she had shown her parents the note after all. She could never fool Mrs. Rogers. Kids don't make initials the same way grownups do.

"They don't mention anything here about calling for an appointment. Do you think they will?"

Slowly Jessie let out her breath, being careful not to make a sound. She had been right. Mrs. Rogers was so dumb she didn't know anything. "They didn't say anything about an appointment," she said truthfully. "They didn't say a word."

"Well, all right, then." Mrs. Rogers smiled at her. "You can go to lunch now. I am sure that we won't have any more trouble like this again. Will we?"

Jessie shook her head and ran out of the classroom.

That afternoon they had assembly. They had assembly every Monday. Assembly was supposed to be a big treat, but usually it was just boring. Either there was an old fat businessman telling them how he used to be a kid at Carver Elementary, or else the principal announced new rules. Today Mrs. Hummers, a second-grade teacher, was standing on the stage waving her arms trying to get her class to sing "Row, Row, Row, Your Boat." Mrs. Hummers loved rounds. She even loved the word *round*. She said it puckering up her lips as though she was sucking on a pit . . . *rooouunds*.

This was going to be the most boring assembly in history. Most of the teachers disappeared right after the pledge of allegiance. The only one who stayed was Mr. Henry, the boys' gym teacher.

Mrs. Hummers was getting all red in the face and she was flapping her arms around like a turkey trying to take off. Then Jessie heard the boys in front of her giggling. They were all flapping their arms like Mrs. Hummers. Some of them were making bird sounds. Then she saw something else.

Mr. Henry was coming up the aisle, looking really mad. The kids in front of her were so busy trying to keep from laughing out loud that they didn't see him.

"Psst," she warned them. But they didn't hear her. Hoping that Mr. Henry wouldn't catch her, she leaned forward and shook Gary's shoulder. He turned around.

"Mr. Henry" was all she had time to say. She sat back quickly in her chair. It was too late. Mr. Henry was standing over them, hissing. He always did that. Jessie couldn't tell if he had seen her or not. He was yelling at everybody.

As soon as Mr. Henry went back down the aisle, the whole class started giggling again. Kenny started imitating him. Mr. Henry whirled around and glared at them, but he didn't do anything. He was busy yelling at another class instead.

Up on the stage Mrs. Hummers tapped her baton for quiet and announced, "We will now sing 'Frère Jacques.'" She looked very happy about it.

Jessie groaned. Another round. She would never live

through this assembly. All the kids in front of her were joking and laughing.

When Mr. Henry's back was turned she reached over and pinched Gary. He seemed a little surprised. Then he passed her pinch on down the aisle.

A little later, somebody started passing a secret along the whole row. By the time it got to her it was so jumbled up and she was giggling so hard she could hardly pass it on.

This was turning out to be the best assembly period she could remember. She thought of a great tongue twister to pass down the row. She leaned forward to whisper it to Gary. Just then she saw Mr. Henry heading up the aisle again. He was looking straight at her. She pretended she was tying her shoe. She held her breath as he came toward her. She tied a double knot. He walked right by and went up to the class at the back of the audi- torium. She started to giggle. Gary reached around and pinched her. She pinched him back.

Jessie went over to Nancy's house after school that afternoon. Nobody was home, so even though they were supposed to be doing their homework, they didn't. They went into Mrs. Helms's room and tried on her jewelry. It was lying all over the place, so she would never be able to tell that they had moved it. After they had on earrings and necklaces and bracelets they decided to practice putting on makeup. After all, soon they would be old enough to wear it and they wanted to be ready. Even though Mrs. Helms never seemed to put makeup on, she had tons of it in all different colors. They tried everything. They were going to paint their toenails but there wasn't time. Jessie was already late for family hour.

She scrubbed her face and ran down the street to her house. She opened the door. It was quiet. Maybe her parents had gotten stuck in traffic and wouldn't even know she was late.

Then she heard her mother's voice. "Jessica?" She sounded funny. It was hoarse, as though she had been crying or something. "Jessie, come here."

"Where are you?" Jessie called.

"Here. In the bedroom," her mother answered. Slowly Jessie went upstairs to her parents' room. Her mother was in bed. Her eyes were all red and she had a tissue in her hand. She couldn't be crying because Jessie was a few minutes late. She must have found out about the note.

"Oh, Jessie!" her mother cried. "I'm so glad you're home."

Jessie was confused. Why would her mother be glad to see her if she knew that she had bad behavior? Maybe it was because her mother wanted to punish her for fighting at school.

"I feel terrible," her mother said.

"Why?" Jessie asked, even though she already knew.

"I have the flu!"

"Is that all?" Jessie asked, relieved.

"Is that all? How can you say that?" her mother

moaned. "I feel terrible. My nose hurts and my throat hurts and my stomach hurts and my body hurts. How can you say 'Is that all'? You are an unfeeling child." Then her mother burrowed way under the blankets. That was what she did whenever she got sick. Jessie and her father were used to it. She wasn't a very good patient. She complained a lot and you had to take very good care of her.

"What do you need?" Jessie asked.

"Maybe some ginger ale would be good for my stomach," her mother whispered weakly.

Jessie brought the ginger ale and sat down on the bed while her mother drank it.

"Was it good?" Jessie took the glass.

"Yes, but now I want something else," her mother said.

"What?" Jessie asked patiently. Sometimes even mothers could act like babies and there was nothing you could do about it.

"Ice cream," her mother decided. "Chocolate."

"Okay." Jessie got up to go to the kitchen.

"Wait!" her mother said. "Maybe vanilla would be better for me."

Jessie knew what it was like to be sick, so she gave her mother some of each flavor.

"You're a good girl," her mother said happily, and settled down to eat her ice cream. Then Jessie moved the T.V. into the bedroom so her mother could watch it.

It wouldn't be fair to tell her mother about the note now, not while she was so sick and weak.

When her father came home, he and Jessie made dinner. Then they sat in the bedroom and watched movies on T.V. until Jessie's bedtime.

✎ SIX

"JESSIE, MRS. ROGERS SAID. "YOU HAVE OVERDUE library books. You have to take them back at lunchtime."

"Okay," Jessie said, heading out the door to the cafeteria.

"Before you eat lunch," Mrs. Rogers added.

"Oh, all right," Jessie said impatiently.

By the time she had returned her books and gotten her food, there was no place left at Nancy's table. She looked around. There was plenty of room next to Gary and Kenny because everyone knew they were too disgusting to eat with. She sat down. Gary and Kenny didn't notice because they were busy mushing their food around.

"I hate meat loaf. Everybody in this school hates meat loaf," Kenny was saying.

"Everybody in the *world* hates meat loaf!" Gary said. He was trying to flip his meat loaf over in the air and catch it, but he missed and it fell on the table.

"It tastes like liver," Kenny said.

"It tastes like cardboard," Gary said.

"And the gravy is green." Jessica giggled.

"Is it?" Gary asked, looking at her plate. His gravy was all mushed with potatoes and carrots so it was kind of orange.

"Green gravy," moaned Gary. "Gross!"

"You can't eat that," Kenny told her.

"Well, what should I do with it?" Jessica said, stabbing it with her fork. Her fork bounced right back at her. "Look at that!" she said. She tried to poke it again.

"Maybe it's made of rubber," Kenny said, getting interested in her meat loaf. "Mine is liver and his is cardboard and yours is rubber."

"We could play catch with it," Gary said, poking it. It was too bad her cousins Billy and Charley weren't here.

They could have a great time.

"Maybe we should take it to shop class," Kenny suggested. "We could make a tie rack out of it."

"There's no such thing as a rubber tie rack," Gary pointed out.

Kenny flipped Jessica's meat loaf up with his knife. It landed on Gary's tray. And it really did bounce.

"Let me try," Gary said. He flipped the meat loaf with his knife. It landed on the floor with more of a splat than a bounce, but it was still in one piece. He picked it up and put it back on Jessie's tray. It left a big green gravy spot on the floor.

"Hey, that's great," Kenny said. "Let's see if it can bounce up from the floor back to the table." He picked up his knife for the attack.

"Wait a minute!" Jessie cried. "It's my turn. It's my rubber meat loaf." She waved Kenny and Gary's hands out of the way with her fork.

"Hey, Nancy!" She called across the lunchroom. Nancy looked at her. "Here comes the bouncing meat loaf."

"Jessie!" Nancy yelped, as the meat loaf sailed across the room.

"Great throw!" Kenny shouted.

Jessie watched the meat loaf bounce off the edge of Nancy's table and splash her with gravy. Then it slid across the floor, leaving a big greasy trail behind it. It finally stopped moving right at the feet of Mr. Henry, who was in charge of them at lunchtime. Mr. Henry didn't seem to think it was very funny. Nobody said a word. A couple of kids giggled and then it got very quiet.

Mr. Henry looked at the meat loaf. Then he looked at the gravy on the floor. Then he looked at the gravy on his shoes and the cuffs of his pants. Then he looked across the room — straight at Jessica.

"Young lady," he said. "What is your name?"

Jessie played kickball that afternoon and tried not to think about Mr. Henry. She concentrated on the game. She concentrated so hard that she was late for family hour. Her parents were waiting for her. They did not look happy.

"Who is Mr. Henry?" her father asked.

"Oh," Jessie said.

"I would like a bit more of an answer," her mother said quietly.

"He's the boys' gym teacher," Jessie explained.

"Since we know you don't take the boys' gym class, it seems reasonable to assume that he is something else as well," her father said.

"He's the lunchroom monitor," Jessie mumbled. "And he hates me. He is very prejudiced. Maybe he doesn't like girls."

"Jessica," her mother said, without even listening to her, "did you or did you not throw your meat loaf at Mr. Henry today?"

"No," Jessie answered.

"Are you saying that Mr. Henry made up this entire

story and called us for no reason at all?" her father asked.

"I didn't throw it. It bounced," Jessie told them. "I didn't mean to bounce it at him."

"Jessica," her mother said very slowly, "meat loaf does not bounce."

"This meat loaf did," Jessie explained.

Her mother shook her head. "You are not an infant, Jessica. An adult does not throw — or bounce food, ever. Do you understand that?"

"But adults have good taste. They don't eat rubber food." Jessie thought that was an excellent point.

"You could have left it on your plate. Did you ever consider that?" her father asked.

"All I did was poke it with a fork. It just jumped up right off the plate," Jessie protested.

"All by itself?" her father asked.

"Almost," Jessie mumbled.

"We are very disappointed in you, Jessica," her mother said sadly. "We thought that you were growing up, and then we find out you've done something completely childish."

"I am growing up. But you won't even listen to me! You just take Mr. Henry's side because he's the teacher. Did you ever think that he might be wrong and you might be wrong and I am right?" Jessie ran out of the living room, up to her bedroom, and slammed the door.

She waited for them to follow her and yell at her some more, but they didn't. She almost wished they would, even though she knew she was right. They didn't talk to her for the rest of the night.

"Do you have the telephone number where we'll be?" her mother asked. She and Jessie's father were going to a plumbers' convention.

"You gave it to me about three times. I practically memorized it," Jessie answered.

"Well, Mrs. Helms has it, too, in case you lose it," her mother assured her.

"Mom, I have the number! I already told you!"

"Well, we'll only be gone for a week," her mother mumbled.

"I know, Mom." Jessie sighed. Her mother was acting as if she were going to China or someplace like that, when she was only going to Chicago.

"We'll drop your stuff off at the Helmses' on our way to the airport," her mother said.

Jessie pushed down on the suitcase so her mother could close it.

"You told me that twice already."

"Are you sure you have everything you'll need?"

"I am only going to be a block away. If I forgot anything I can come back and get it," Jessie pointed out as patiently as she could.

"Are you sure you'll be okay?" her mother asked for the twentieth time.

Jessie didn't even bother to answer.

"Remember to tell Mrs. Rogers that you are staying

with the Helmses," her mother said. "Maybe I should call her myself."

"I can do it," Jessie said.

"Well, honey —" Her mother turned and looked at her. "I'll miss you."

Jessie hugged her mom, but just for a second. Otherwise her mother might have started crying or something.

"I'll miss you, too," Jessie mumbled. It was true, but mostly she was thinking about how much fun she would have staying with Nancy.

They waved good-bye, then Jessie went to school.

"Book reports are due," Mrs. Rogers reminded them just before lunch. "Everybody who hasn't turned theirs in yet, leave them on my desk on the way to lunch."

Jessie's stomach tightened. She had forgotten all about her book report. Well, maybe not exactly forgotten, but she just hadn't had time. She could do it tonight. Mrs. Helms wouldn't care how late she stayed up and if she was only one day late Mrs. Rogers wouldn't mind. She ran out of the classroom to the cafeteria.

It was definitely more fun staying with the Helmses than it was at Jessie's house. It was also a lot noisier. There seemed to be more things to do at Nancy's. Jessie's mother always cooked dinner almost by magic, but Mrs. Helms needed a lot of help and it took a long time, so dinner was about an hour later than it was at Jessie's. No wonder Nancy had learned to do her homework so quickly. There was hardly enough time to do it at all. Of course, Mrs. Helms let them stay up later than Jessie did at home, but they were both so tired they fell asleep before she told them to go to bed.

"Remember that we'll be home late on Wednesday, Mom," Nancy yelled as they were about to go to school the next morning.

"Sure," Mrs. Helms said. "I remember that but I forget why."

"We have our class trip," Nancy said impatiently. "Why don't you write notes to yourself or something?"

"I don't need to. You always tell me everything twenty times," Mrs. Helms answered.

The class trip was to the museum. It was supposed to be educational, but it was mostly going to be fun. Maybe Mrs. Rogers didn't know that, but nobody told her, just in case. They would see rocks and dead birds and snake skins and arrowheads and stars and the bones of old dinosaurs. Everybody in the class had been talking about it for days.

"Jessie," Mrs. Rogers called as they were going to the cafeteria. "I want to talk to you."

"What is it?" Jessie asked, coming back.

"Where is your book report? It was due yesterday. Everybody in the class has turned theirs in except for you," Mrs. Rogers said.

"I bet they haven't," Jessie said. "I bet Ben hasn't. He

doesn't even know how to read."

"Jessica. That is very rude! I don't know what is happening to you but I don't like it one bit," Mrs. Rogers said, blowing her nose. "You started off the year so well."

It was easy for Mrs. Rogers to say that. Nobody called *her* a teacher's pet. Nobody called her P.M.R., short for Perfect Mrs. Rogers. Jessie didn't want to be like Mrs. Rogers, and if Mrs. Rogers didn't like it, that was too bad. Because now all the kids in her class liked her a lot and that was much more important.

Mrs. Rogers went on. "This isn't the first time, Jessica. During the past few weeks your homework has grown sloppier and sloppier. Several times you haven't done it at all." Then she looked up. "I think we have to do something about this, don't you?"

That was one of those teacher questions that you aren't really supposed to answer. After all, what was so important about a book report? She had read the book and that was the important thing. But she knew that you can't say that to a teacher, so she didn't say anything at all. She just looked down at her shoes.

"Jessica, look at me," Mrs. Rogers said.

Jessica couldn't, because she knew if she did that she would start yelling and get into even more trouble.

"What do you think we should do about all this missing work?" Mrs. Rogers asked again.

"I'll do it," Jessie mumbled.

"That's exactly what I thought, Jessie," Mrs. Rogers said. Jessie had come up with the right answer. "That is why I am afraid that you will not be allowed to go on tomorrow's trip to the museum. You are going to have to stay here and make up the work that you have missed. Is that perfectly clear?"

Jessie stared at Mrs. Rogers. "That isn't fair!" she howled.

"Maybe not, but what you have been doing isn't fair, either. It isn't fair to yourself not to do your homework."

Now that was really stupid.

"But I want to go on the trip." Jessie tried again.

"I am afraid, Jessie, that you can't do the things that you want to do if you don't do the things that you are responsible for as well. You may go to lunch now." Mrs. Rogers looked down at the papers on her desk and began to read.

Jessie couldn't tell Nancy what had happened. Even though Nancy wasn't the teacher's pet or anything like that, she always got pretty good grades. It was just that her parents didn't expect her to get a perfect report card so they were always really happy when she got A's. Jessie's parents were the other way around. They expected her to get good grades, so when she did they didn't even seem to care.

If she told Nancy about how she couldn't go on the class trip, Nancy might tell her parents and they might call Jessie's parents. They would be furious. They would make her come home after school every day and do homework for hours for the rest of her life.

Maybe Nancy wouldn't even notice that she wasn't on

the trip. And if she did, Jessie could say that she had a headache or something and was in the nurse's office when the bus left and missed the trip. Then Nancy would just feel sorry for her.

All that night the only thing that Nancy could talk about was the trip. Jessie wished she would just shut up. She had never noticed before what a loud voice Nancy had. It could really get on your nerves.

"What's the matter with you?" Nancy asked as they went to bed. "You haven't said a word all night."

"How could I?" Jessie answered. "You talked so much there wasn't time."

"Well, good night to you," Nancy said, and she turned her back and went to sleep.

Jessica lay awake for hours. She just couldn't fall asleep. Sometimes her eyes would close, and then they would pop right open again. That kept happening all night long.

"Is something the matter, Jessie?" Mrs. Helms asked her the next morning.

"No," Jessie said quickly.

"I hope you aren't getting sick," Mrs. Helms said. "You look pale."

"No," Jessie said. "I'm fine."

"Let's make sure we get a seat at the front of the bus," Nancy suggested as they walked to school.

"No," Jessie said.

"Why not?" Nancy looked really hurt.

"I just feel like sitting alone," Jessie said.

"Well, go ahead," Nancy said angrily, and she ran up the steps to school.

Jessie walked down the hall very slowly. Maybe all the other kids would have left by the time she got to her homeroom. Then nobody would know that she couldn't go on the trip. But when she got to the door she could hear all the kids yelling. They were really loud. Slowly she went inside. A spitball hit her on the arm. She looked up. Kids were running all over, and Gary and Kenny were jumping around making their dinosaur noises. A blonde woman Jessie had never seen before was sitting at Mrs. Rogers's desk — a substitute.

"Would you all please settle down!" she yelled.

Nobody paid any attention.

"Shut up!" she yelled.

Everybody turned. They had never heard a teacher tell kids to shut up. Teachers were supposed to set good examples.

"Mrs. Rogers has the flu and can't go with you on your trip today. My name is Miss Williams and I am going with you instead. The buses are waiting, so would you please line up quietly so we can get moving."

Everybody ran for the door. Jessie waited to see if Miss Williams would say anything to her, but the substitute was too busy trying to get everybody lined up. Jessie decided she should just get on the bus with everybody else.

She was sorry that she had told Nancy she wanted to sit alone. It would have been much more fun to sit with somebody, but it was too late now, and anyway the bus ride was pretty short.

They ran up the stairs to the museum shrieking as loud as they could. Miss Williams kept trying to line them up to count them about every five minutes, and every time she got a different number. Finally she just gave up.

"If any of you get lost and miss the bus, I bet your parents will be glad," she growled. Jessie didn't think she was a very good teacher. Teachers were supposed to like kids. Miss Williams didn't seem to like them at all.

On the first floor there were glass cases filled with little Eskimo dolls. They were supposed to be fishing and hunting for seals. They were pretty boring except when they were killing the seal and there was fake blood all over the place. That was disgusting. Everybody stared at it until Miss Williams yelled at them to move on.

Then they went through a long hall with glass cages full of stuffed animals and fake trees and plants. The animals were supposed to be drinking water and eating grass, but they were really all stuffed and dead. When they got to the fake monkeys, Kenny and Gary started jabbering like chimpanzees and Ben started thumping around like an ape. Miss Williams grabbed them and dragged them down the hall to the next room. She was pretty strong.

Right before lunch they went to the dinosaur hall. It was so big you could hear your voice echo. There were dinosaur skeletons all over. One was so huge it reached up to the ceiling. It even had teeth. It was called *Tyrannosaurus rex.* The only thing it didn't have was skin. Of course, skin makes a big difference.

Nancy leaned over the red velvet rope and touched its tail. All the tiny bones rattled. It was scary.

Ben and Kenny and Gary came running over. "It's alive," whispered Ben in a fake spooky voice.

"Get away from here," Jessie warned. "You'll break something."

"How do you know?" Ben growled.

"You're as clumsy as a baboon," Jessie shouted back.

"I am not. I bet I could climb to the top." Ben gestured to the dinosaur's head, about fifty feet up in the air.

"I dare you," Jessie said.

"I double dare you to do it, too," Ben answered.

"Okay," Jessie laughed.

"No!" whispered Nancy, so the guard wouldn't hear them. "You'll break it."

"You don't understand about doing scary stuff, Nancy." Jessie tossed her head.

Jessie slipped underneath the rope and grabbed on to the tail with Ben. Suddenly, the bones began to shake. Jessie looked up at the giant dinosaur head. She hoped that the whole thing wasn't going to fall down right on top of them. She tried to hold the tail to keep it from shaking, but it wouldn't stop. Then, a tiny bone fell off the tip of the tail right onto the ground. She picked it up and tried to stick it back on.

Ben ran and crawled outside the rope. "You did it, Jessie! I didn't even touch it. It's all your fault!"

"You are such a liar, Ben," Jessie started to yell, when the two big hands of a guard grabbed her and lifted her into the air.

The guard practically carried her out to the bus while Miss Williams followed, screaming the whole time. The chief guard and the head of the museum said that they would never let a fifth-grade class from Carver Elementary School inside the museum ever again.

✎ SEVEN

MRS. ROGERS SAT IN FRONT OF THE CLASS, BLOWING HER nose loudly and yelling. She said she had been forced to leave her sickbed because of them. Then, even though she always said homework wasn't punishment, she gave them about fifty pages of math to do and made them write a composition on how you are supposed to behave when you go to museums and other cultural places.

Jessie took out her notebook and started writing.

"Jessica and Ben," Mrs. Rogers called out. "Come up to my desk."

They stood there in front of her, looking down at the floor.

"The two of you will now go to the principal's office and explain your reprehensible behavior to him," Mrs. Rogers announced.

"But nobody ever told us we couldn't touch the dinosaur," Jessie protested. "We shouldn't have to go see Mr. Grasse for that."

"Nobody ever said you shouldn't jump off a cliff, either," Mrs. Rogers pointed out. "There are some things that we expect you to be able to figure out for yourselves."

Jessie and Ben didn't say a word all the way to Mr. Grasse's office. They sat on a bench in the hall and waited. The door opened.

"Ben Carney," Mr. Grasse called.

Ben went inside and the door closed. Jessie wondered what was happening inside. She wished that Mr. Grasse would yell at them together. It would save time, and she wouldn't be so scared. After a long time Ben came out, but before Jessie could ask him anything Mr. Grasse called her name.

"Jessica, I have been looking over your record," he began. Jessie didn't even know she had a record. It made her sound like a criminal. Wait till her parents found out about that. "Until this year you have been an excellent student," Mr. Grasse went on. "But something seems to have happened. Your parents have been notified of your behavior by both Mrs. Rogers and Mr. Henry." He paused as though he expected her to say something, but she didn't know what. She couldn't tell him about what she had done with the note. "Not only did you behave badly at the museum yesterday, but you knew perfectly well that you were not supposed to be on that trip at all, didn't you?"

Jessie nodded.

"Mrs. Rogers had told you to stay in school and make up missing assignments, hadn't she?"

"But it wasn't fair," Jessie tried to explain. "Lots of kids are late with book reports and they get to go everyplace."

"Jessica, I am not interested right now in other kids. I am interested in you," Mr. Grasse said. "I am sure that your parents will feel the same way."

"No, they won't," Jessie said. "They don't care about behavior."

"I think they will care this time, Jessie."

"I'll ask them," she agreed sullenly.

"I think this time I will ask them, Jessie. Please understand that this is for your own good," Mr. Grasse said.

"Don't," Jessie shouted. She didn't mean to shout, but she had to or else she would cry.

Mr. Grasse looked at her for a long time. Jessie was afraid that he was mad at her for yelling. But when he spoke to her his voice was very soft, as though he was trying to be nice.

"Why?" he asked. "Why are you so worried about my calling them?"

How could she tell him her parents would hate her forever if they found out? He wouldn't believe her. So she just shrugged.

"I am going to suggest to your parents that we all meet and discuss this situation. That way we can help you and your parents," Mr. Grasse continued.

"My parents don't need help," Jessie mumbled.

"Well, I am going to call them and find that out. I just want you to know that, Jessica, so that you don't feel this is all happening behind your back," Mr. Grasse explained. "You may go, Jessie."

There was nobody in the hall when Jessie left the principal's office. That was lucky because she was starting to cry and she didn't want the other kids to see her.

This was really terrible. Even though everyone else finally knew that she wasn't perfect, her parents still thought she was. That was why they loved her. They told everybody how perfect she was. They would never forgive her. She hadn't wanted *them* to know she wasn't perfect, just the kids at school and people like that. If her parents stopped loving her, she would die.

She went out to the playground. All the kids were waiting. Ben was with them, and so was Nancy.

"What happened?" Ben asked. "Did he yell at you, too?"

"Did you get into trouble?" Nancy asked.

"He really screamed at me," Ben bragged. "He said I

could never go on a school trip for the rest of my life."

"Did he give you a note?" Nancy asked.

"No," Jessie said. "He's going to —"

Then she remembered. He couldn't call her parents because he didn't know where they were. She had never told Mrs. Rogers that they were away. She had forgotten and nobody knew. She was safe. Her parents might never find out after all. Suddenly she felt so happy that she started to cry.

"Oh, Jessie," Nancy said. She thought that Jessie was crying because the principal had yelled at her. She didn't know that Jessie was crying in relief. "Don't worry. It will be okay. Just stop crying or your eyes will get red and my mother will know something happpened. I won't tell her anything, and soon everyone will forget about it."

"Do you think they will?" Jessie asked.

"I'm sure of it," Nancy reassured her. "But you'd better not do stuff like that again, ever."

"I won't," Jessie said. "Ever."

"So now you are going to be teacher's pet again," Ben shouted. "I knew it."

"Just shut up," Jessie screamed.

That night Jessie did all of her homework very carefully. She even did extra work. Maybe she could go back to being perfect. Maybe everything would be all right. She had to stay up really late to finish, but it was worth it.

The next day, even though she had turned in her book report and had done all her homework, a monitor came into their classroom and gave Mrs. Rogers a note.

"Jessie," Mrs. Rogers said. "Mr. Grasse wants to see you."

She followed the monitor to the principal's office. Once she had wanted to be a monitor, but now she knew that she never would be one. They only let kids who didn't get into trouble be monitors.

"Jessica, I have been trying to reach your parents," Mr. Grasse said. "I have called your house, but nobody has been home. I have also left messages at your father's office, but he hasn't returned my calls."

"Well, they have very busy lives," Jessie explained.

"I am sure that they do, Jessie, but this is a very serious matter. Have you explained that to them?"

"Yes," Jessie lied. "They know that."

"They don't seem to understand that we are seriously concerned with what is going on with you, Jessica."

"I know," she mumbled.

"I hope that they do too," Mr. Grasse said.

Jessie didn't say anything.

"If they don't come in and speak with us, I don't think we can promote you to the sixth grade next year, Jessica. It isn't that you have failed your work, but we are worried about your attitude."

Jessie looked at him. He was just trying to scare her.

"Perhaps you are not mature enough for the sixth grade. Your parents don't seem to realize that. If failing to promote you next year is the only way we can make that clear, then we will have to do that. Do you understand?" Mr. Grasse asked.

"Yes," Jessie said, even though she didn't. Everybody had always said she was very mature for her age. Mr. Grasse must be making a mistake.

"I will keep trying to reach them, Jessica, but you have to explain to them that they will have to make an effort as well."

Jessie went back to her classroom, but she didn't say a word to anybody. Nancy tried to talk to her but Jessie pretended that she didn't hear. When they got to the Helmses' house she started doing her homework immediately and just ignored Nancy. Nancy finally stopped trying to talk to her.

When it was time for dinner she couldn't eat anything. She tried, but her stomach was all clenched up and nothing could get inside. Finally, she finished her work and went to bed. But she couldn't sleep. She kept tossing and turning and her stomach kept hurting. She must have made a noise or something because suddenly the bedroom door opened and Mrs. Helms came in. She knelt down next to Jessie and put a hand on her forehead.

"Is something wrong?"

"I feel sick," Jessie moaned softly. It was true. She had been feeling sick ever since she talked to Mr. Grasse.

"What's wrong?" Nancy asked in a sleepy voice.

"It's all right," Mrs. Helms said gently. "Go back to sleep, Nancy."

Nancy shut her eyes.

Mrs. Helms got Jessie a glass of water and then sat on her bed while Jessie drank it. "I think you'd better not go to school tomorrow. Okay, Jess?"

"Okay," Jessie said. She did feel a little better. She was so glad she didn't have to go to school tomorrow she almost started crying again.

As soon as the door closed, Nancy opened her eyes.

"You should have said you were sick instead of not talking all day."

"I was too sick. You don't understand about sick people," Jessie explained. "You're too healthy."

Jessie stayed home the next day. Mrs. Helms said she still looked a little green around the gills, but Jessie figured that must be a joke because people don't have gills, fish do.

That night Jessie's parents came home. She could hear them talking to the Helmses in the living room while she packed her suitcase. Even though she knew that Mrs. Helms didn't know about Mr. Grasse, she was still worried. She packed as fast as she could.

"Oh, Jessie," her father said as he hugged her. "We're so sorry that you're sick."

"I knew I should have stayed home with you," her mother said sadly.

"Oh, no!" Jessie said. Then she explained quickly, "I would have gotten sick anyway."

"I guess so," her mother said. If they knew the truth, they wouldn't be so glad to see her. They might not have come back at all.

"Poor baby." They both hugged her again. She let them, even though she wasn't a baby, because it might be the last time they would ever hug her in her whole life.

When they got home they put Jessie to bed as if she were still a little kid. She wished that she still were.

Her mother wouldn't let her go to school the next day. Jessie was glad, because she never wanted to see Mrs. Rogers or Mr. Grasse again. She and her mother played three games of checkers and Jessie won twice. Her mother even read her a story, which she hadn't done in years, and it was really nice. Her mother was an excellent reader. They made chocolate pudding, which her mother said was the best thing for sick stomachs, especially if you lick the spoon. Then they watched all the quiz games on T.V. and guessed the answers before the people on the program. They would have won $41.123.00 if they had been playing for real.

About six o'clock her father came home. He was really upset. Jessie could tell because he just slammed the door and took off his coat without saying a single word. "Come down here!" he shouted.

Suddenly Jessie's stomach dropped and she got very queasy. Her father had found out about Mr. Grasse calling his office. He knew.

"Trudy eloped!" her father bellowed as loud as he could. He started pacing around the living room. "She's been planning this for weeks!" he shouted. "She hasn't done a stick of work. The files are a mess! And she lost every single telephone message from last week!"

"What?" Jessie looked up.

"Every single one!" her father sputtered. "Orders from customers — everything. Nobody knows who called or what they wanted or anything."

"That's great!" Jessie yelled. She couldn't help it.

"What is great?" Her father looked shocked. "What is great about your father going broke?"

Jessie's mother put her arm around his shoulders.

"You know you're exaggerating, George. You aren't going broke."

"Maybe," her father agreed reluctantly. "But I still want to know what is so great."

"I'm happy for Trudy," Jessie explained quickly. "I bet she was a beautiful bride."

"*Harrumph*," her father said, and he flopped down on the couch.

The next day she went up to Mrs. Rogers and handed her the note that her mother had written.

"From your parents, Jessie?" Mrs. Rogers asked.

Jessie nodded.

Mrs. Rogers read it. "But this is your excuse for being out of school, Jessie. Isn't there anything else your mother wanted to say?"

"No, ma'am," Jessie said very politely. From now on she was going to be very polite to Mrs. Rogers.

"Well, all right, Jessica. You may take your seat."

Even though all the kids were screaming and making noise, Jessie sat very quietly in her chair being very well-behaved. A couple of times she saw Mrs. Rogers glance at her and she tried to look as perfect as possible. Maybe it would be all right after all.

The end of school came faster than it ever came before. When Jessie got to school on the last day, kids were running around the room taking things down off the bulletin boards, emptying out desks, and putting stuff in shopping bags.

Finally everyone got quiet and Mrs. Rogers made a little speech about how much she had liked having them in her class that year. Then she told them that she hoped they would all work really hard next year in the sixth grade. Jessie was relieved. Mrs. Rogers hadn't said that *some* of them would have a good time in the sixth grade. She had said *all* of them.

Then Mrs. Rogers walked down the aisle and handed out their final report cards. Everybody around her was screaming and comparing grades.

"Jessie, what room are you in next year?" Nancy asked.

"What room are you in?" Jessie asked her.

"Six-oh-three," Nancy said. "And so is Gary!"

"Me too!" Kenny said.

Very slowly Jessie turned over her report card. She could see the heavy black printing: THIS STUDENT IS PROMOTED . . . And there, written in red ink it said: 5th Grade, Room 505. She couldn't believe it. She looked again. It was true.

"What's the matter, Jessie?" Nancy asked.

"I'm not in your room." Jessie spoke very softly so that Nancy couldn't hear how her voice was shaking.

Nancy looked disappointed. "We can still play at recess and after school."

Nancy was trying to make her feel better, but Jessie could only nod; she couldn't say a word. It felt like something was caught in her throat.

"Hey," Nancy said. "Maybe you should go to the principal and see if you can change. Maybe if your parents wrote a note . . ."

Jessie wished Nancy would stop being so nice.

"Who wants to be in your room anyway?" she shouted.

Nancy looked hurt, but Jessie was afraid if she didn't scream she would start to cry.

Then she saw Mrs. Rogers coming down the aisle toward them. She hoped Mrs. Rogers wouldn't say anything — not now, not in front of everyone.

"Mrs. Rogers, I'm sick," she said quickly. It was true. Her stomach was turning over and over. "I have to go to the nurse." Jessie put her hand over her mouth.

Mrs. Rogers looked at her sadly. "Okay, Jessie. Nancy, you go with her."

Jessie ran as fast as she could. She made it to the nurse's office just in time.

"She'll be all right," she heard the nurse tell Nancy. "I'll call her parents."

✎ EIGHT

JESSIE'S PARENTS WERE SO WORRIED ABOUT HER GETTING sick that they didn't even ask about her report card that night. They seemed to have forgotten about school completely. But Jessie couldn't. Her parents told her to rest and not to worry about anything, but she couldn't help it. Finally, after her parents had fallen asleep, Jessie got out of bed and took out her report card.

With the red pen, very carefully and breathing very hard while she did it, she changed the five in "5th Grade" to a six. Then she changed the room number, so that it said "605" instead of "505." Then she went back to bed. She felt better. Even if her parents never asked to see it, she would never have to look at that report card again.

The next day her parents asked her if she would like to visit her grandmother. They thought that would make her feel better. It did. She got so excited about the idea that she completely forgot about her stomach and everything.

Her grandmother was a great cook and she let Jessie help in the kitchen. She had a huge house with lots of rooms that were filled with boxes and boxes of all kinds of old clothes and pictures and magazines and stuff like that. She let Jessie look at everything and didn't care if she put things back in the wrong place. Maybe that was because there really wasn't a right place for anything. Her grandmother kept saying she was going to organize all her things and throw a lot of the old junk out, but she never did, and Jessie knew she never would.

Her grandmother also liked to go places, like to the museum or the zoo, or to the park to watch fireworks. Almost every day they went someplace different.

After a couple of weeks it was time to go home and start rehearsals for the play. Jessie had been reading and reading her script. She had practically memorized the whole thing, all the parts — even the boys' — so she was really ready.

On the morning of the first rehearsal Jessie ran over to Nancy's house. Mrs. Helms was going to drive them because Jessica's parents worked all day. When Jessie got there she found Nancy's mom on her hands and knees under the coffee table. Mrs. Helms looked up.

"Hi, Jessica. Are you feeling better?"

Jessie nodded and grinned.

"You didn't happen to notice my keys, did you?" asked Mrs. Helms, crawling out from under the table.

"I found them, Mom!" Nancy called from upstairs.

"Where were they?" Mrs. Helms asked as Nancy came in waving the keys.

"In your green shoe," Nancy said.

"Yesterday I left them in the refrigerator," Mrs. Helms told Jessie. "I can't imagine why." Neither could Jessie.

"You should get extras," Jessie advised her.

"I did. Now I have three sets of keys and I keep losing all of them," Mrs. Helms said, shaking her head.

"Mom, we're late," Nancy urged.

"All set!" Mrs. Helms said cheerfully. "But now where are the keys?"

Jessie picked them up off the coffee table where Mrs. Helms had just put them, and they all got in the car.

For the first week of rehearsals everything was so confusing and there was so much to do that Jessie didn't even have time to think. At family hour she told her parents about all the funny things that happened during the day, and everything seemed almost the way it used to be. She didn't tell them how Mrs. Helms had put the car in reverse by mistake and backed into a fire hydrant. She wasn't sure they would understand, even though she knew they liked Nancy's mom very much. Mrs. Helms was a college teacher, and Jessica's father always said that she was the absent-minded professor. Her parents thought that was okay because they said she was brilliant. Jessie sometimes wondered if Mrs. Helms had become a college teacher just because she was so absent-minded.

The hardest part for Jessie was the dancing. She and Nancy had to practice every afternoon after rehearsal. Nancy would stand and scream "One! Two! Three! Four!" and Jessie would try to get her feet where they were supposed to be. But they never seemed to end up in the right place. She put in extra steps all the time. *She* knew what she was supposed to do — but her feet didn't. Finally, Mrs. Helms cut out a bunch of cardboard feet and Nancy put them on the floor. Jessie just had to get her feet into the footprints before Nancy called out the numbers. It helped a little.

But nothing could help Nancy's singing. Jessie and Mrs. Helms made a tape of the music that Nancy could play over and over in her sleep. Mrs. Helms said you could learn a foreign language in your sleep if you did that, but it didn't work on Nancy's voice. She did know all the words, though.

When everybody sang together, Nancy just mouthed the words. But when time came to give out the solos, Nancy was terrified. Mr. Rhimsky was standing in front of the chorus with his baton. When he pointed at you,

you were supposed to sing all by yourself. Everybody was scared, but Nancy was scared the most. Then Mr. Rhimsky pointed to her.

Jessie held her breath. Nancy was just terrible. Mr. Rhimsky looked as though he couldn't believe it. He asked Nancy to sing again. It was even worse. He pointed at her a third time. But just as she opened her mouth, very wide, he changed his mind. He pointed at Jessie instead. She was so surprised at being asked to sing that she didn't even have time to be scared. She sang perfectly. Mr. Rhimsky stared at her and actually smiled. Then he glared at Nancy. That made them start to giggle. Then he glared at them both.

The next day he assigned the solos and Jessie got one. It was short, but it was a real solo and she also got one line to say. She couldn't wait to tell her parents. She knew how proud they would be. It was the first time she had really looked forward to family hour for months.

Her parents were getting more and more excited about the play. Her mom volunteered to make costumes for both girls because Mrs. Helms said that sewing was one of the things you couldn't do if you were absent-minded. She said that everything she sewed came out backward and inside-out at the same time.

"Stand up straight, Nancy, so I can fit this," Jessie's mother said, her mouth full of pins. "You are getting to be so tall. You're already two inches taller than Jessie." She turned and looked at Jessica. "You are going to be like me, I'm afraid. Short." Jessie felt guilty. Maybe she should have grown faster. But her mother was laughing. Jessie looked at her closely. Her mother didn't seem to mind that Jessie wasn't tall. It seemed to be okay.

The orchestra didn't come to rehearsals until five days before opening night. They were so noisy that you couldn't hear anybody singing at all. Gary and Kenny both played trombones. They were so horrible that Mr. Rhimsky made them sit in the very back row where no one could hear them.

Nancy loved that rehearsal because she could sing as loud as she liked and nobody heard. She sang so loud she got red in the face. Jessie was giggling so hard at Nancy that she couldn't sing at all. Everybody was running around, but nobody seemed to know where to go. Even Miss Shaw gave up trying to shout directions from the audience and just sat down and laughed at the confusion. Jessie thought that being in a play was the most wonderful thing that could happen to a person, and she knew that everybody in the cast felt the same way. It was like having a very big, very noisy family.

She and Nancy came skipping out of the auditorium at the end of the rehearsal. This evening Jessie's mom was picking them up. Jessie could see her in the dark, standing next to the car.

"What a beautiful night," her mother said. "You can see so many stars." Jessie and Nancy looked up. There must have been a million. "And it smells so nice." Jessie and Nancy took deep breaths. "You can almost smell the fall coming," Mrs. Fowler said, getting into the car. "It's hard to believe the summer is almost over."

Jessie started to feel sick on the drive home.

Time started to go very fast. Suddenly it was the night before the opening of the play and they were having dress rehearsal, where everybody wore their costumes for the first time. Jessie's mother was very worried about Jessie and Nancy's costumes. She made them both try everything on about twenty times and stuck both of them with pins trying to get them to fit. She even accused Nancy of growing between the first time she tried on her costume and the second time. They had to explain to her that kids don't grow an inch in three days. It was funny to see her mother so worried, trying so hard to be perfect. They were really beautiful costumes, even if the hems were a little bit crooked. When Nancy danced, her skirt flipped around and looked really great. Jessie didn't know if hers did because she still had to look at her feet.

The only problem was that the closer they got to the opening, the closer they got to the end of the play, and the closer they got to the end of the play, the closer they got to the beginning of school. And there was no way to stop it. Jessie tried not to think about it. But her stomach knew. It hurt all the time now.

They had to go to the auditorium very early on opening night, so Jessie spent the afternoon at Nancy's house. Her parents would come to the play after work.

Nancy wanted to practice her singing one more time, but Jessie and Mrs. Helms wouldn't let her. Jessie didn't have to practice because she had finally learned all of the steps in all the dances. Mrs. Helms kept telling them to relax, but they couldn't. Nancy talked all of the time; she couldn't shut up for a minute.

The more she talked, the worse Jessie felt. She hoped that they would just go out and leave her alone for a minute so her stomach could calm down. But everyone just kept on chattering. Jessie clenched her teeth. Maybe that would help. It didn't.

Mrs. Helms looked at her and said calmly, "You're turning green again, Jessica. Are you going to be sick?" She asked it just like an ordinary question, as though she were asking Jessie if she wanted a glass of milk. Jessie started to laugh, but that was a mistake. The minute she unclenched her teeth, terrible things happened. She barely made it into the bathroom. Mrs. Helms followed her. Nancy wanted to come, too, but Mrs. Helms wouldn't let her.

Jessie just kept throwing up. Mrs. Helms was very nice. She was even funny, but that only made it worse. Jessie just got sicker and sicker. Finally Mrs. Helms made her drink a glass of water and then she hugged Jessie very, very tightly. She wrapped Jessie up inside her arms. And then Jessica started to cry. She cried very hard for a long time. Mrs. Helms didn't say anything. She didn't tell Jessie to stop, and she didn't tell her that there was nothing to cry about. She just hugged her tighter than ever, and finally Jessie was quiet.

"Don't tell my mother," she finally whispered.

"Don't you think if you are sick she would want to know?" Mrs. Helms asked gently.

"I went to the doctor. He said my stomach was nervous," Jessie explained.

"I see," Mrs. Helms said. Then she hugged Jessie again. It seemed dumb, getting hugged when she wasn't sick and she wasn't crying anymore. But she didn't want to hurt Mrs. Helms's feelings. Then after a minute she started liking it. She sort of leaned against Mrs. Helms. She was starting to feel sleepy.

"Why don't you lie down for a few minutes, Jess," Mrs. Helms suggested, even though Jessica hadn't yawned or anything. She led Jessie to her own bed and pulled back the covers. Jessica got in and Mrs. Helms sat down next to her.

"How did you know I was sleepy?" Jessica asked as her eyes shut.

"You can tell a lot when you care about someone," Mrs. Helms said.

Jessie's eyes popped open. Then she realized that Mrs. Helms didn't know — she couldn't. She wouldn't be this nice if she knew.

But Nancy's mom kept looking at her. "I once told you that if you ever wanted to tell me anything, you could." She sat next to Jessie on the bed. "You still can. I won't tell anyone. Not Nancy and not your parents. Do you believe that, Jessie?"

Jessie nodded. She wanted so much to believe her. She opened her mouth but the words just wouldn't come out. She started to cry. Mrs. Helms looked down at her.

"It's hard, isn't it?" Mrs. Helms said.

Jessie nodded again.

"Do you want to try and tell me now?" Mrs. Helms asked.

"I can't," Jessie whispered.

"Okay," Mrs. Helms said and got up to leave. Then she turned back and got on her hands and knees and started looking for a book under the bed.

"Sorry I made such a mess," Jessie mumbled.

Mrs. Helms just smiled. "Nothing that can't be cleaned up," she said, bumping her head on the bed. Then, rubbing her head, she left the room.

It was amazing, Jessie thought as she fell asleep, that even when she was being sick and crying and everything, Mrs. Helms didn't seem to care. She still liked her — even when she was being disgusting. But before she could think about it anymore, she was asleep.

Nancy came in to wake her. She was trying to be quiet but she couldn't.

"Wake up, Jessie!" Nancy hissed at her. "Hurry up! It's time! It's opening night!" She started to dance around the room.

"I told you to wake her gently, Nancy," Mrs. Helms said. "I hope you don't want to be a doctor or a nurse when you grow up. You would drive your patients crazy."

But Nancy didn't care what her mother said. She was bouncing around the room, and she was trying to sing again.

"She's giving me a headache," Mrs. Helms complained to Jessie. But Jessica's stomachache was all gone. In fact, she felt pretty great.

Mrs. Helms was so excited that they were halfway down the driveway before she noticed Nancy wasn't in the car.

"Now, did we forget anything?" Mrs. Helms asked as they pulled out of the driveway the second time. She looked at Jessica and Nancy. Jessie giggled.

In fact, Jessie felt like giggling at everything. She was sitting squished between Mrs. Helms and Nancy, and whenever one of them laughed they could feel each other's shoulders jiggle, and that made them all laugh again.

"I was in a play once," Mrs. Helms told them as they drove to the auditorium.

"Were you good?" Jessie asked.

"I don't think so," Mrs. Helms said, but she didn't seem to care. She was smiling. "In my first scene I was supposed to exit through the front door."

"What happened?" Nancy asked.

"I was sort of nervous and so I walked into a closet by mistake."

Nancy giggled. Jessie started to giggle, too. Nancy's mom laughed loudest of all.

"Wait. I'm not finished. I slammed the door shut and it

got stuck. I couldn't get out of the closet! I banged and banged at the door. I shook it as hard as I could."

"What happened?" Nancy and Jessie both shrieked at the same time.

"Well, somehow that knocked down whatever was holding up one wall of the set and the whole wall fell onto the people on stage!"

Mrs. Helms laughed so hard she had to stop the car.

"Mom!" said Nancy. "That's a terrible story to tell people just before a play."

"Do you think so?" Mrs. Helms looked worried. "I didn't mean to make you nervous."

"You aren't very sensitive," Nancy said.

"It's okay." Jessica tried to reassure Nancy's mother. "There aren't any doors in this play."

"Oh, good." Mrs. Helms looked relieved.

The dressing room was already full of people. The older kids were running around looking for costumes and making jokes, as if there were nothing to be nervous about. Nancy and Jessie started to put on their makeup but they weren't sure where to put the lines. Both of them wound up looking like Jessie's grandmother. Finally an older girl came over and helped.

Miss Shaw came in and told them they were going to be marvelous. She told them to "light up the sky." Jessie and Nancy weren't quite sure what she meant by that.

Then the music started. Before Jessie knew it, the stage lights went on, the curtain went up, and there she was — right in front of the audience. At first she was afraid that she wouldn't be able to move. Then things started to go really fast. Suddenly it was almost time for her line. What if nobody laughed? But they did, and it was the loudest laugh in the whole show. Then the scene changed and the dancers came and went, and before she knew it, everyone was clapping and they were all bowing.

Miss Shaw and Mr. Rhimsky came backstage and they were crying and kissing everybody. Jessie folded her costume neatly and put it away, but she left her makeup on. It felt too wonderful to take off.

Suddenly Mr. Rhimsky shouted for everyone to go back onstage. Nancy and Jessie couldn't imagine what he wanted. When they got there, the scenery was leaning up against the back wall of the auditorium and there were big tables on the stage with food and punch and soda. It was their first real cast party. Last year they had been too young to stay up that late. It was fantastic. Everyone was laughing about mistakes they made or dumb things that went wrong. Jessie and Nancy listened, amazed. It seemed to them that the performance had been perfect.

Before they knew it, it was almost midnight.

"Are you girls ready to go yet?" Mrs. Helms asked them.

"Are you leaving?" said a voice behind them. They turned around and Mr. Rhimsky and Miss Shaw were standing there.

"Good-bye, both of you," Miss Shaw said. "I hope I'll see you next year. You are two very talented young actresses."

Miss Shaw kissed them on both cheeks. Jessie and Nancy turned bright red. Miss Shaw shook hands with their parents and congratulated them on having such talented daughters. Jessie couldn't believe it. Even though she couldn't dance without cardboard footprints, she was talented.

They sang songs from the play all the way home. Jessie knew all the words, but sometimes her parents had to just hum along.

When her parents kissed her good night, her mother gave her an extra hug. "Tomorrow we'll go and buy you a new dress for the first day of school."

✎ NINE

WHEN THEY GOT TO THE DEPARTMENT STORE, HER MOTHER headed right for girls' clothing. Jessie tried to get her interested in other things on the way, but it didn't work. Her mother said that she didn't need a hat, and her father had plenty of ties.

Then her mom looked at her for a minute.

"Is anything the matter, Jessie?"

"I'm thirsty," Jessie said.

"Okay. Let's go get a Coke."

After they sat down, Jessie looked at her mother's face for a long time. She was a very kind-looking woman. Maybe Jessie could tell her, after all. It would feel really good. Just then the waitress came with her Coke and her mother started talking about what kind of dress they were going to buy. Still, all Jessie could think about was telling her. She could practically feel the words coming out of her mouth.

"Mom . . ."

Her mother looked at her. But the words couldn't get out. They just stuck there. It actually hurt.

"What is it, Jess?" her mother asked.

"Let's go to the girls' department," Jessie said. She took her mother's hand, the way she had when she was little.

She couldn't even look at the dresses. She just kept feeling the words she was trying to get out of her mouth.

"Can I help you?" asked the saleslady, just as Jessie's mouth was opening.

"We're looking for a dress," her mother explained to the saleslady. "For my daughter."

"I see. And what does the young lady have in mind?" asked the saleslady, whose name was Gloria. She was wearing a badge that said so.

"Something not too fussy," Jessica's mother said.

"What grade are you going to be in?" Gloria asked.

Jessie couldn't say a word.

"The sixth," Jessie's mother finally answered for her.

"Really?" said the saleslady. She sounded as though she didn't believe it. "You must be very smart," she went on.

"You don't have to be smart to be in the sixth grade," Jessie told her. "Plenty of kids in the fifth grade are smart, too."

"I'm sure they are," Gloria agreed. "They do grow up quickly," she said to Jessie's mother. Mrs. Fowler smiled proudly.

Jessie hated this saleslady.

"Well, why don't you try these?" Gloria suggested.

The saleslady kept coming in and out of the dressing room, and each time Jessie could feel the words she wanted to say to her mother slipping back further and further in her mouth, until she knew that she couldn't say anything at all.

When the first day of school came, Jessie still didn't know what to do. Maybe something would happen to her. Maybe she would be attacked by a pack of wild dogs. But she wasn't. By the time she got to school, the last bell had rung. Everybody else in Room 505 was already there.

The teacher's name was Mr. Courtland. He wrote his name on the board. He printed it because some of the kids in the fifth grade couldn't read script very well yet.

"Oh," he said when she went up to him. "You are Jessie Fowler."

She nodded.

"Well, take a seat in the back."

She had never sat in the back before. That was because she was usually one of the short kids in the class. But this time she was about the tallest. She was a giant compared to all these kids.

The teacher started handing out books for the year. Jessie had already read them. She already knew everything in them. They might even be hers from last year.

All the kids around her were looking at her in a funny way. She didn't know any of them. After all, they had only been in the fourth grade last year.

Then the teacher went around the room and made everybody stand up and say who they were. Jessie tried to shrink down behind her desk so that nobody would notice she was there, but it didn't work. They got to the kid sitting in front of her, and then it was her turn. Everybody was waiting. She couldn't stand up, she just couldn't. Her knees wouldn't hold her. She leaned on her desk and mumbled her name. She hoped that nobody would be able to hear her. For one awful minute she was afraid Mr. Courtland would make her repeat her name louder. She could see everyone in the room staring at her. A couple of the kids even started to laugh at her. She knew they would. After all, she was a dummy. She had been left back. But Mr. Courtland just nodded at her and went on to the next row.

Then he started talking about what they would learn this year. Jessie didn't pay any attention because she already knew everything you did in the fifth grade. She was worrying about what she would do at lunchtime. Suppose Nancy and the other kids saw her come in with a fifth-grade class. They wouldn't let her sit with them, and she couldn't sit with these babies.

When the lunch bell rang, she practically ran out of the classroom and hid in the girls' room. It was pretty crowded, but nobody she knew was there. All the other girls were talking about their new classes and their new teachers. Everybody sounded really happy. Everyone else in the whole school was excited. Jessie listened until they left. They were all going to the lunchroom.

She couldn't go. She couldn't even go out in the hall. What if one of the little kids from her class started talking to her? And what if one of her old friends saw that? Then she looked out of the funny frosted window in the door to the girls' room. She could hear everyone laughing and the dishes clanking all the way from the cafeteria. She could even smell what they were eating — meat loaf. Even rubbery meat loaf would be delicious.

Finally she heard the next bell. It was the end of lunch period. She hurried down the hall and back into Room 505 before anyone could notice her.

In the afternoon Mr. Courtland talked about all the school trips they were going to take to places Jessica had gone to last year. She didn't want to go again. The teacher handed out permission slips for their parents to sign. How could she explain why all her trips were to places she had already visited?

Mr. Courtland just kept handing things out. Jessie didn't even look at most of them, she just put them neatly away in her desk. She was glad she was at the end of the row. At least she didn't have to turn around to pass anything on. She didn't have to look anybody in the face.

It was the longest first day of school that Jessica had ever had. It seemed to last forever. She thought maybe the bell had broken or something. But finally it was over.

She got up to go. Then she sat back down. If she left now, everybody she knew would be in the school yard. They would want to know what room she was in and where she had been all day. And how could she tell them? She would have to wait until everybody went home. She waited until she couldn't hear anybody outside anymore. Then she waited another few minutes just to be sure. She went out of her classroom, down the hall, and out of the school. It seemed to be safe. Then she saw Nancy walking back toward her.

She jumped into the bushes next to the path and pulled some of the branches over her head. They got stuck in her hair. She couldn't see anything. She couldn't hear Nancy's feet because she was wearing her new running shoes. She held her breath.

Then she heard a huge crashing-around in the bushes. She looked up. Nancy's face was staring down at her.

"What are you doing, Jessie? Are you crazy or something?" Nancy was asking. Nancy kept asking questions while she pulled Jessie out of the bushes. Jessie didn't want to come, but Nancy just kept on pulling.

"Jessie, you tore your new dress!" Nancy said, shocked, even though she had spilled chocolate milk all over her own new dress.

Jessie looked down. It was true. She had jumped into a thorn bush. Her dress was dirty and her arms were scratched.

"Jessie, what is it?"

Jessie tried to say that nothing was wrong, but instead she started to cry, right in front of Nancy.

"You can tell me, Jessie. We're best friends."

She did. She told Nancy everything. When she finished, she looked down at the ground.

"So now I guess you will want a new best friend," she mumbled.

"Don't be stupid, Jessie. Best friends don't have to be in the same grade, you know," Nancy said, punching her in the arm.

Jessie couldn't believe it. Nancy wasn't just trying to make her feel better. She meant it.

"When are you going to tell your parents?" Nancy asked. She made it sound perfectly possible; she seemed to think that Jessie could do it.

And Jessie really wanted to. She hoped she could.

"Do you want me to come with you?" Nancy asked, just as though she could read Jessie's thoughts. "They can't yell at you too much if I'm there."

Jessie looked at her friend. "Please."

Jessie's mother was already home when they got to her house. Maybe she could tell her mother, and her mother could tell her father.

"Jessica!" her mother said looking at her. "What happened to you? Look at your dress."

"Hi, Mrs. Fowler," Nancy said, to distract her.

"Hello, Nancy. Jessie, what happened?" Her mother looked worried.

Just then her father came home.

"Isn't that your new dress?" her father asked as he came in.

"A pack of wild dogs chased me," Jessie said desperately. If they got mad at her about her dress, what would they do to her when she told them about being left back?

"Jessie!" Nancy said.

"What is going on?" her father asked.

Nancy poked her in the ribs. It was time. She opened her mouth. Nothing came out. Her parents looked at each other. She tried really hard. The words were right inside. She could almost reach them. She tried as hard as she could. She started to choke.

"Jessie, what's wrong?" Her mother looked frightened.

Then, without any warning, Jessie started to cry. She tried to talk, but she couldn't. All that came out was an awful sound — like a baby crying.

"What?" her mother said. "What is it, honey?"

"I . . . I got . . . into . . ." and then the words got all jumbled up in her crying.

"She says she got into trouble," Nancy explained.

"What kind of trouble?" Her father looked very worried.

"Are you hurt?" her mother asked.

Through her tears Jessie tried to tell them.

"She got left back," Nancy finally had to translate.

"What!" her mother and father said.

Jessie could only nod.

For a few minutes nobody said anything, not even Nancy.

"Thank you, Nancy," Jessie's mother said. "I know you care about Jessie, but now I think we have to have a private talk."

"No!" Jessie hugged Nancy.

"It's okay, Jessie," Nancy told her friend. "It's just your mom and dad." Then she left.

Jessie's father got up and went into his den. Jessie sat very quietly looking at her mother. After a few minutes her father came back.

"I called the school," he said. "I spoke to the principal." He turned to look at Jessie. "He told me everything that happened last year." Then in a soft voice he told the whole story to her mother. All of it. It took quite a long time.

Her mother looked at her sadly. "I don't understand, Jessica. This just isn't like you."

"It is too!" Jessie started shouting. She hadn't meant to; it just came out that way. "Nobody else has to be perfect. Everybody can do homework in the closet except for me. Everybody else can watch television. It isn't fair. Why can't I be like everybody else? If you really loved me, you wouldn't make me be different."

She was crying so hard now that she couldn't talk anymore. She had wanted to cry like this all summer, but she couldn't. Now the tears just kept coming out.

"I just don't understand you, Jessica," her father began.

"I know you don't," Jessie said, still crying. "That's the whole problem."

"Wait a minute," her father interrupted. "Are you saying that all of these things happened because of us?"

"You think I'm this little baby, this cute little baby who is always perfect — and I'm not!"

"That's obvious," her father commented.

"Let her talk," Jessie's mother said. She was sticking up for her, after all. Jessie began crying again.

"It made me different from all the other kids," Jessie tried to explain. "They made fun of me."

"We don't care about the other kids, Jessie. We care about you," her father said. He said he cared. But he just sounded angry.

"*I* care about the other kids!" Jessie said.

"But you have to be yourself," her mother explained. "You have to do what you believe in."

"But you don't really mean that," Jessie wailed. "You mean that I should do the things that *you* believe in. And you believe that I am this little baby who never makes any trouble."

"We do know that you are growing up, Jessie," her father said. "And we certainly are learning that you get in trouble . . ."

"The fact of the matter is you *are* somewhere in

between being a baby and being a grownup," her mother explained quickly.

"I am much more grown up than you think I am. I have real problems, but you don't believe that!"

"What kind of problems?" her mother asked.

"Well, like being the teacher's pet," Jessie said.

Her father sighed.

"You see what I mean!" Jessie yelled. "You don't think that's real, but I do."

There was silence. "I'm sorry." Her father looked at her. "I guess I forgot how terrible it is to be called the teacher's pet. Do you believe me?"

Jessie didn't answer.

"Don't you believe us, Jessie?" Her mother looked concerned.

"Why should I? You don't believe me."

"What do you mean?" her mother asked.

"You never listened to my side about Mr. Henry. You just figured that because he is the teacher I was a bad little kid. But maybe I was right. And you never even listened."

"What was there to listen to? You did throw food and you were rude," her father said. "You did something wrong. We couldn't ignore that, could we?"

"But I didn't do it on purpose. I didn't throw food at him. It was an accident! We were having a protest. You don't know how bad our food is! You never asked me if the meat loaf was rotten or anything — and it was green. If I had eaten it instead of bouncing it I would have died of ptomaine poisoning. Did you ever think of that?"

"No," her father said, "I have to admit I never did."

"I think there might be a better way to protest," her mother said gently.

"Well, maybe," Jessie said.

"We're getting off the point. It isn't the food, it's your behavior," her father said. He sounded angry again.

"Nobody likes to be teased for being the teacher's pet. But you didn't choose a very intelligent way of dealing with it," her mother said.

"What would you have done?" Jessie asked sullenly.

"You could have come to us," her father suggested.

"No, I couldn't," Jessie said. "Because you think it's good to be the teacher's pet, and I don't."

Her parents looked at each other.

"What about Mrs. Rogers's note?" Her father changed the subject. "You lied to us about that."

"I know," Jessie mumbled.

"What made you do that?" Her mother sounded worried. "I really want to know."

"I didn't want you to be mad at me," she whispered.

"We wouldn't have been that mad," her father said. "Not as mad as we are now."

"And you wouldn't have had to go through such a terrible summer," added her mother.

Jessie looked away from her.

"Don't you think that we would have helped you?" her mother asked.

"I don't know," Jessie muttered.

Her mother looked upset. "But we love you, Jessie."

"Even when I'm not perfect?"

"Don't be ridiculous!" Her father started to shout again but her mother put a hand on his arm and he stopped.

"You are always telling everyone how perfect I am and how that's why you love me . . ." Jessie's voice trailed off.

"Oh, Jessie." Her mother was crying. Jessie had never made her cry before. "That's not true. We love you."

"And we never really thought you were perfect," her father said.

"Really?" Jessie looked up, surprised.

Her mother smiled at her. "Everyone knows that nobody is perfect. We know that you make mistakes, but they don't matter. That's what growing up is, Jessie — making mistakes and fixing them."

"And if you thought that we could ever stop loving you, honey," her father said, so quietly she almost couldn't hear him, "then we made a pretty bad mistake, too. Do you think we can fix that?"

"You mean you really still love me, even though I'm in bad trouble?" Jessie asked.

Her parents nodded.

"You promise?" She looked right at them.

"We promise." Her mother hugged her really hard. They both started crying again, but this time it was because they felt so much better and loved each other more than ever.

"Actually, I think we are all in trouble," her father said.

"What do you mean?" asked Jessie.

"Mr. Grasse wants to talk to the whole family," he explained.

"We all have to go to the principal's office," her mother said.

"Well, maybe if we all go in and explain that we have learned a big lesson, we can straighten everything out," her father suggested.

"And he won't think that I'm too immature for the sixth grade."

"And we aren't too immature to be the parents of a sixth-grader," her mother added.

"I bet we can convince him," her father said.

"Come on, Jessie!" Kenny yelled. "Score!"

"We're winning, we're winning!" Nancy was screaming as she went running toward home plate while Jessie crossed second base.

"We're ahead! Hooray for Jessica!" Kenny shouted.

The minute Jessie kicked the ball she could tell it was going to be great. She could just feel it and now they were going to win the game. Because of her!

Everybody was screaming by the time she got back to home plate. They had won the championship. They were the best kickball team in the entire sixth grade! And she had scored the winning run. This was the best thing that had happened to her in her entire life. She felt even better than she had after Mr. Grasse let her go into the sixth grade with all her friends.

Kenny was pounding her on the back. Nancy and Gary were jumping up and down with excitement.

"Come on, Nancy," she said after they stopped celebrating and it was beginning to get dark. "I have to get home, so if you're walking with me, we'd better go."

"Okay," Nancy said. She started looking all over for her books. "But after I do my math problems, can I call you up and see if I got the same answers?"

"Hey, how come you don't tell me if *my* math is right?" Kenny asked, walking along with them.

"Because you aren't my best friend," Jessie said. She gave Nancy a very special smile.

"But your homework is always perfect," Kenny complained.

"Not all of it," Jessie said truthfully. "Just the math."